WHAT WAS A TERRIFIC CAR LIKE THIS DOING IN A TINSEL TOWN LIKE LAS VEGAS?

The Corvette was stolen.

Stolen from the high school that owned it.

Stolen from the boy who had rebuilt it from scratch and turned it into a work of art on wheels.

Stolen by a man who could have bones broken with a snap of his fingers and didn't mind the exercise at all.

Now the boy was coming to get his car back.

And not all the muscle in Vegas, or all the allure of the lovely girl who offered him a delicious detour, was going to keep him out of the driver's seat. . . .

Great Movies Available in SIGNET Editions

*Price slightly higher in Canada

If you wish to order these titles, please see the coupon at the back of this book.

Corvette Summer

A *novel* by
WAYLAND DREW

from the original screen play
by Hal Barwood
and Matthew Robbins

A SIGNET BOOK
NEW AMERICAN LIBRARY
TIMES MIRROR

Published by
THE NEW AMERICAN LIBRARY
OF CANADA LIMITED

NAL books are also available at discounts in bulk quantity for industrial or sales-promotional use. For details, write to Premium Marketing Division, New American Library, Inc., 1301 Avenue of the Americas, New York, New York 10019.

Copyright © 1978 by The Plotto Company

Photographs from the MGM release CORVETTE SUMMER © 1978, Metro-Goldwyn-Mayer, Inc.

First Signet Printing, June, 1978

1 2 3 4 5 6 7 8 9

 SIGNET TRADEMARK REG. U.S. PAT. OFF. AND FOREIGN COUNTRIES
REGISTERED TRADEMARK — MARCA REGISTRADA
HECHO EN WINNIPEG, CANADA

SIGNET, SIGNET CLASSICS, MENTOR, PLUME AND MERIDIAN BOOKS are published in Canada by The New American Library of Canada Limited, Scarborough, Ontario

PRINTED IN CANADA

COVER PRINTED IN U.S.A.

Corvette Summer

Chapter One

———◆———

Kenny Dantley never dreamed.

When he was fifteen and had fallen off the roof of the trailer and broken his arm, his mother decided to ask the doctor about several things bothering her about her son. "What the hell," she said, as the taxi dropped them at the emergency entrance of the hospital, Kenny cradling the bent limb, "while we're here we might as well have him look at your toe, and your ear, and those teeth you say hurt sometimes."

The duty intern had set the arm and cleaned the accumulated wax out of Kenny's ears and, after frowning at what he saw inside the boy's mouth, recommended a dentist as soon as possible.

"One more thing," his mother said. "The kid says he never dreams. Am I supposed to believe that? I mean, *everybody* dreams, don't they?"

The doctor shook his head and frowned. "It could just be, Mrs. Dantley, that Kenny dreams but doesn't remember. Probably that will change as he grows up." He paused. "If I were you, I wouldn't worry too much about *that*."

Kenny waited but his mother said nothing else, and they had gone home to the trailer, and his mother had changed back into her slacks and poured herself three fingers of Cutty Sark because, she said, she needed it.

She forgot to take him to the dentist; a year later he went himself and had the teeth pulled out.

Three years had passed since he broke that arm. He had waited to dream, or at least to remember that he

1

dreamed, but it had not happened. Each dawn when he awoke he waited to remember. He pushed out of his mind all the images that had already begun to crowd upon it, and he tried to recall where he had traveled in his sleep, and whom he had met, and what adventures he had had. But there was nothing. Nothing. Between going to bed and waking there was nothing at all, not even a void, or a chasm, or a gulf, or anything that could be described by those fancy words that Forrie Redman, the English teacher, was always telling them to use. There wasn't even darkness. There was just ... nothing. Zilch. Blotto. Zip.

And so it was on the dawn of this hot day. He opened his eyes only long enough to see light in the room, then he shut them tight and thought about remembering; but between going to bed and waking up there lay only the familiar blank. *What the hell*, he thought. *I guess I'm just not old enough. Maybe it'll start when I get laid*. He stretched his lanky arms behind his head. He grinned. He knew that if somebody had been lying in bed with him she would see the gaps where teeth had been, and he didn't care. He waited a moment longer to make sure that everything was right, and then he opened his eyes.

He really didn't mind not dreaming, because whenever he wanted to he could dream with his eyes wide open, fully awake. At will he could summon visions to blot out all the disagreeable realities that surrounded him—the chipped, gray kitchenette table; the vase of dusty plastic daisies; the stained ceiling and the bleached drapes puffing a little in the hot morning air; the trailer itself; the way his mother looked every morning; the mile of tacky streets between home and school; English class; history class; math class. At will, he could summon images to erase all misfortune that the world might thrust on him. There was no limit to the custom work available in his imagination, and every morning it began here in this cubicle that was his bedroom, stacked with car magazines and well-

2

thumbed customizing books, lined with posters, decals, and color photos of engines, cars, and myriad automotive details perfect to the last, twentieth coat of lacquer and to each chrome-plated bolt head.

He exhaled slowly. There they were, as reliably and breathtakingly beautiful as ever—Trans Ams, Camaros, Firebirds, Mustangs—a profusion of models and colors from which Kenny Dantley's imagination drank every morning, drank deeply, and satisfied a profound thirst for beauty. With the delicate touch of an artist he had imaginatively dismantled and rebuilt each of these cars at least a dozen times. Effortlessly once again, luxuriously as he awoke, he juggled gear ratios, torques, engine and carburetor potentials. He considered brake possibilities, transmissions, shocks, clutches, manifolds, and overdrives. Names like Weber, Shiefer, Weiland, Holley, Offenhauser and Koni drifted through his mind like old friends. He toyed with mag wheels and wire wheels. He considered rubber—would it be Goodyear or Goodrich or Uniroyal?—and finally, fully awake, he began to redesign the bodies, flattening and broadening, fitting scoops that matched perfectly the symmetry and proportions of the whole phantom car. He molded spoilers that swept gracefully back in flares across the fenders and vanished into lean flanks, only to reappear arching over the rear wheel wells.

He suspected that, seen from the front, his cars would command a touch of fear as well as respect, for there tended to be something threatening about their low grilles and broad, dark windshields. His profiles were very low, very long, accentuated by the best Hooker or Thrush sidepipes and by a paint job that stressed the horizontal, the solid, and marked the machine unmistakably as a Dantley custom job. In these waking dreams he saw men stopping in the street, reaching out to draw their companion's attention, saying, "I think . . . yes. Yes, it *is*! Look at that: It's a Dantley!" And his car would pass with the ineffable

3

grace of a creature that had nothing, absolutely nothing, to prove.

Restraint. That was the key to a master paint job. Restraint, depth, tireless polishing, *gloss*. It would be the paint job that distinguished his cars every time. Mechanically skilled though he was, he knew that almost anyone could fit together the components of a major muscle car. Hell, even Kuchinsky could probably do that, given enough time! But no one he knew could match his finesse with a pin-striping brush, or the understated elegance of his painted designs. All the cars that glided soundlessly through Kenny's imagination were made beautiful, finally, by artistic touches that were inimitably his own.

His mother groaned; he felt the trailer move as she rolled over in her bed. She was waking up. Very soon she would call him weakly, her face half buried in her pillow, and ask him to bring her a Bromo and some aspirin, and when he had done that she would say, "Oh, Jesus, what a head! Could you get breakfast, Kenny? Could you put some stuff in the blender? Could you do that for your mother?"

Soon, but not quite yet. He had five minutes yet to think about the car, *his* car, the car he would someday own. For this car, a machine which was still forming in a separate part of his imagination, an entire wall had been reserved, a wall across the top of which was written in impeccable Old English script,

Kenneth W. Dantley, Jr.

He allowed his head to turn, now, and he looked at that name approvingly. The job had taken two full days—two days of tracery so grueling that when he had finished he couldn't stop his eyes from watering and there wasn't enough strength in his left arm—his painting arm—to lift a Coke. But it had been been worth it. The name radiated dignity, authority. It

4

would look good on letterheads and on business cards like the ones Mr. McGrath kept under the glass top of his desk. His name was the one thing in the world that was unquestionably his, and he had long ago decided to make the most of it. The inscribed wall was at least a beginning.

Of Kenneth W. Dantley, Sr., his father, he knew only one fact for certain: That in 1960, when he had abandoned his wife and son, he had been nineteen. Dantley's mother had some yellowing, out-of-focus snapshots that showed him as a crew-cut kid, grinning, clowning, leaning against a gleaming white front fender that was itself so beautiful that sometimes when his mother wasn't home Kenny took the photos out to look at that one snapshot—his father and his father's car. "He was fun-loving," his mother had told him once when she was drunk. Then she hadn't spoken for several minutes; she had just sat on the edge of her bed and moved in a way that Kenny had seen Australian aborigines move in a film about funerals—rocking very gently, gripping their knees.

"Don't cry," he said.

"I'm not crying," she said. "I wouldn't cry for that sonuvabitch."

He noticed creases in her neck that he had never seen before. "Tell me more," he said.

"More? What more? He liked good times. He liked to travel. Jeez, the man was *made* to travel. So, for a little while, we traveled together, that's all."

"Then I came."

"Yeah. Then you came and we couldn't move so easy anymore. So he left."

"You hear from him?"

She shook her head slowly, shoulder to shoulder. "Nope. Not a word. Eighteen years, and not a single goddamn word!"

"It was a Corvette, wasn't it, that you moved around in."

"Yeah. Get me a drink, Kenny, and I'll tell you something."

He had gone and poured the drink for her and brought it back. She had fallen backward onto the bed. "You were going to tell me something," he said. "Here."

She propped herself up, reaching. "That car," she said. "That was one helluva gorgeous car."

"Yeah." He was thinking about it. A 1959. He knew every detail of the cockpit—red vinyl, it would have been, and red broadloom. He knew every detail of the engine also, because General Motors was still sending *The Corvette News* to Kenneth W. Dantley, and he had been careful, whenever they had moved, to send the change of address. He had sent changes of address often over the last few years. He was wondering what such a car would cost now, meticulously restored at the Dantley shop. He was grinning.

"But that's not it," his mother was saying. "That's not what I wanted to tell you. What I wanted to tell you was that I was *jealous* of that car." She began to laugh, and then she covered her face so that Kenny could not tell whether she was laughing or crying. Then, little by little, dabbling with a kleenex at her eyes and nose, she got control of herself. "Can you imagine that? But it was *so* beautiful, and when we drove through a town people would stop and look. And they never did that to me. Um-um. Never. He loved that bloody car. And in the end it was the car that took him away, wasn't it, so I was right to be afraid of it." She lowered herself back onto the bed, sighing. Kenny took the glass away and then slipped her shoes off and swung her feet up under the blanket.

"And you'd still like to be with him, wouldn't you? Even now."

But there had been no reply. She slept.

In the splendid gallery of Corvettes that adorned Kenneth W. Dantley, Jr.'s, favorite wall, the 1959 stock model occupied a place of honor. But it was by no means alone; in fact, every Corvette ever manufactured was represented there. And it was to this particular wall that, no matter where he was, in moments of stress and tension, Kenny Dantley drifted away in his imagination. Ultimately, when he could afford that luxury, his customizing shop would handle nothing but Stingrays. He could see them now, gliding off the highway . . .

The trailer moved. "Kenny?"

Slipping across the asphalt like big easy cats . . .

"Kenny?"

. . . temperamental cats; their throaty purr threatening at any moment to become a snarl, a roar, a surge of vocal energy to match . . .

"Kenny?"

. . . the power thrusting back through the drivetrain. In his dreams, Kenny Dantley drove all the cars with consummate ease, comfortable with that power. And at his side, sometimes, there was a beautiful woman. . . .

"Kenny? Kenny!"

"Yeah."

"You see what time it is?"

"Yeah."

"You're gonna be late. Hurry up. I don't want a call from the school. Hear?"

"Yeah. Okay."

"And bring me some orange juice or Coke or whatever's there, will you? Jesus, I feel awful!"

"Okay."

Someday, thought Kenny Dantley, beginning to clothe his skinny form, gaze still fixed on the pack of Stingrays, isolating, finally one that was unique. His car. The vivid image of which would make his dull day bearable. *Someday* . . .

Chapter Two

"Today," Mr. McGrath said, hitching up his trousers. "Might as well do it right now. No point theorizing, is there? I've already made arrangements at the yard. Let's go!" And fitting a cap firmly on his balding head, he led the way out of the shop toward the blue Dodge Maxi van parked in the teachers' lot.

Whooping, belching, roaring, laughing, punching each other in shoulders and kidneys, kneeing one another in the thighs, the class followed. Their shouts were unintelligible. Communication—the exchange of clear ideas between two human beings—was anathema to these students. Communication was what happened in classrooms, and they had failed at it times past counting, and their failure had driven them to a mockery of it with the animal sounds which, among them, frequently passed for speech. Communication was definitely out; noise was in. Sheer, brute sound was much more desirable, mixed whenever possible with violent physical contact. Everything got slapped, punched, or kicked—desks, walls, tires, books, tools, and asses. What followed Mr. McGrath's thickening form into the sunlight was not a class by any stretch of the imagination; it was a mob few teachers would care to confront. And it was a tribute to McGrath's patience and kindness that during the course of the next few months, the first of the school year, he would give them a common project and goal, he would teach these failures to take pride in a job, and perhaps even give some of them a glimpse of attainable excellence.

"C'mon," he shouted. Lessgo! Get the lead out!"

Dantley trailed behind. He was being cautious, not insolent. He knew that the smell of unwashed bodies inside McGrath's van would be almost unbearable, and he intended to ride beside the open back door. Even so, this position was a second choice for him; he would have preferred to ride in the passenger's seat beside McGrath so that they could discuss the various customizing jobs they would be sure to pass on the freeway. But to have raced weeds like Kuchinsky and Kootz for the seat would not have been cool at all.

The van was already moving when he reached it. "For godsake, Dantley," McGrath said, beating his left arm on the door, "Lessgo! Lessgo! Whatya think this is, a picnic?"

"I think it's a goddamn zoo, that's what I think it is," Dantley said, and swung up into the rear.

"Stomp it, sir!" somebody shouted.

"Lay some rubber, sir!"

"Burn up that ramp, Mr. McGrath!"

"Gently, my friends, gently." McGrath waved a soothing hand. "There is no need for me to demonstrate the unbelievable power of this machine." He waited for the raucous laughter to subside. "And besides"—he shut his eyes piously—"I am a law-abiding citizen."

Decorously, with its sweaty, delinquent burden, the van proceeded away from the school, swinging toward the heart of the city, and the tracks.

Dantley rocked with its rhythm, hands dangling between his knees, watching the back of the teacher's head. He was extraordinarily fond of McGrath. If he had allowed himself to think in such terms he would have acknowledged that the shop teacher had become a kind of model for him. He liked him not because he was a teacher, but in spite of it. He knew very well that McGrath had never officially succeeded as a teacher. He drew all the peripheral staff duties like Driver's Ed, Assistant Track Coach, standby dance monitor, projectionist, and so on. In the staff skit at Christmas he was always absurdly dressed, a buffoon. It was clear even to his students that his formal qualifications as a teacher were marginal, third rate, and it was clear to Dantley that since McGrath hadn't made it now, by his mid-forties, he would never make it. He was a genteel failure. He would never be a principal, or an assistant principal, or even a chairman. He was, in fact, lucky to keep his job, because if almost anyone else had wanted it, he would have been out. Like the kids he taught, Ed McGrath was basically a dropout; the difference was that somehow he had hung on. And in material terms he had managed to do remarkably well; Dantley had seen his house.

"Almost there," McGrath said, pointing through the van's windshield. "You can see the crane on the horizon. There."

Ironically, even McGrath's flagrant, genial incompetence had been an encouragement to the kids he taught, because if he had made it in a kind of way, if he had had good luck, then maybe they could too. Maybe, like McGrath, they'd get the breaks. Maybe, like McGrath, some use might be found for them. Maybe, like McGrath, they could find some place where, as long as they could manage to stay, they would not be total losers.

For Kenny Dantley, of course, that place was somewhere inside the fantastic world of cars, inside the magic machines. And it was McGrath who had taken him there first. It was McGrath who had taught him to drive, even bringing his own car for after-hours Driver's Ed because, he said, Dantley had a feel for it. It was McGrath who had taught him all the basic information on engines, transmissions, and bodies, and it was McGrath who had taken him personally to the school library and, under the disapproving glance of the bearded and overweight librarian, run a greasy finger through the card index and shown him how to use the car shelf to find out anything he wanted to know.

10

No other teacher had taken such time with him. No other teacher had shown him how small pieces of knowledge could be fitted together like perfectly tooled components to form a whole "more beautiful than the sum of its parts," as McGrath had once said. In no other subject—English, math, history, whatever—had Dantley discovered anything practical or pleasing to eye, hand, or nose. None of them, in his words, "followed through." But McGrath followed through. McGrath and his students produced beautiful cars.

"Last year," McGrath was saying to the new members of the class as he turned into the wrecker's yard, "we did a Camaro and it was very successful. Wouldn't you say it was successful, Dantley?"

"Car was nice. Ricci's paint job looked like cat shit."

"Sit on it," Ricci said.

"Cat shit in a thunderstorm," Dantley added.

"Okay, okay. Here we are," McGrath was saying. "Now remember, we don't want no foreign cars . . ."

"Let's do a dune buggy," Kootz shouted.

"Asshole," said Ricci.

"And no dune buggies," McGrath said. "What we produce's gonna have a body on it. A classy body. Okay, here we go."

The doors of the van flapped open and spilled the human contents, squinting, scratching, spitting, and punching, out into the rust and dust of the wrecker's yard.

It was a mournful prospect. As far as they could see, shattered automobiles lay strewn on the landscape, some singly, toppled on their sides or backs for easier gutting, some in small groups as if forlornly huddled for safety, some in huge heaps piled by the crane that was even now swaying across this scene of devastation like some presiding monster. The place stank of the hot, dry, crumbling rot of metal. It was alive with groans and sudden shrieks as the stacks sank and readjusted themselves, and as the crane dipped for another carcass and tore it from its resting place. Periodically,

11

from somewhere behind the piles of rusting carcasses, came a grinding more terrible than all the other sounds, so loud that when it occurred Dantley felt the earth shudder beneath his feet.

He stared balefully around. He hated these places worse than cemeteries. "Jesus," he whispered to himself, shaking his head, "all those dreams."

"Ed McGrath from the school," McGrath was shouting to a distant man with a cigar. "Phoned. Made arrangements with Jimmy." The man waved and disappeared inside the corrugated metal shed. "Galaxie . . . Caprice . . . Malibu . . ." McGrath began pointing to various wrecks, shading his eyes as he walked. "Fury—there's a straight one . . . Grand Prix—good doors . . . Matador . . ."

"Let's get it," Kootz shouted. "Let's get the Matador!"

"Shut up, Kootz!" Ricci was staring at him in disbelief. "You've got no taste, you know that? You'd take a goddamn Edsel, if you could find one, wouldn't you?"

"Hey," said Kootz. "Nice car, Edsel!"

Ricci clapped a hand to his forehead. "Kootz, klutz," he said.

"Yeah," said Kootz. "Nice car, Stutz."

"Cutlass," McGrath continued, "GTO . . . Polara . . . Pinto . . . Now there! There's a Mustang 'sixty-six. We could make that a very neat little machine, no trouble at all. Kuchinsky, crawl under there and have a look at the frame."

Kuchinsky was very plump. She wore denim coveralls and a yellow T-shirt that said *Eat a Beaver: Save a Tree*. With difficulty she wriggled through the litter and under the rocker panel of the Mustang.

Ricci leered. "Doesn't usually take ya *that* long to get on your back," he said.

"Up yours, Ricci." Kuchinsky's voice was muffled. "Frame looks okay, Mr. McGrath . . . but hey!, there are no springs at all."

Mustangs were far down on Dantley's list. He'd

12

settle for one if Mr. McGrath said so, but in his opinion the basic car did not justify the work of restoration. He turned away from the group and was heading off to his left in search of something more interesting when he saw it. At first it was only a rising orange shape glimpsed from the corner of his eye, but a shape nonetheless with unmistakable features—the curved fender, the slightly bulging door panel, the elongated snout. Dantley spun, shading his eyes.

A Corvette!

A Stingray!

The front was smashed, the rear was crumpled, the windshield looked like the web of a demented spider, but it was without question a Stingray—a '72, Dantley thought, already beginning to run, maybe a '73—dangling like a doomed fish on the crane's hook, turning as it rose.

"Hold it! Hold it!" By the time Dantley had covered the hundred yards to the scrap heap in front of the crane the car was already descending on the other side, and when he rounded the corner, nearly crashing into the rear of the crane, he saw to his horror what had been making the grinding, earth-shuddering sounds since his arrival. A crusher! Beside it stood a neat stack of 4×4 cubes that had once been cars. Around it lay bits of nondescript debris popped out by the terrible pressures of destruction. Above it, descending into the yawning maw, hung the Corvette.

"Jesus! No! You can't!" Gasping, Dantley flung himself against the side of the crusher, desperately searching for a way up. The car descended, dropped, scraped with a sickening sound into the hopper, and the hydraulic ram began inexorably to close on it. Seconds before it would have been mashed beyond recognition, Dantley reached the cab of the machine howling and beating both fists on the glass. The operator, an impassive negro with a wool watch cap pulled down close to his eyes, turned to discover a grotesque and grimacing face flattened inches from his own. Dantley

13

flung his arms at the car as if he sought to Cradle it safely away. He gesticulated wild-eyed at the control lever clenched in the operator's hands. "Off! Off! Off!"

The man turned the switch. There was sudden silence in the scrap yard except for the cooling sounds of the engines and Dantley's final outburst which rose above the mountain of cars to where McGrath and the rest of the class were still examining the Mustang: "You asshole! Can't you see that's a Stingray? A *Sting*ray!"

"Dantley," said McGrath, looking around. "Where's Dantley?"

They began to look. Singly and in pairs they reached the crusher and clambered up around the hopper to peer down inside. McGrath and Kuchinsky arrived last, puffing. "Oh, God," said McGrath, seeing the solemn faces. "Oh no! Don't tell me the crazy kid's fallen *in* there!"

But what he saw when he looked over the lip of the hopper was an ecstatic Dantley, not a crushed one. The kid was already inside the car, leaning through the right window, gripping an imaginary steering wheel in his left hand. Disheveled, sweaty, filthy, he grinned up at McGrath and pointed to the huge engine revealed by the already open hood. "A 350," he said, smiling blissfully.

Kuchinsky whistled.

"This is the one, Mr. McGrath," Dantley said. "This has gotta be the one."

McGrath spread his hands skeptically. "Fiberglass body?"

"Why not?" Ricci asked.

"Yeah, yeah, why not?" said Kootz.

"Well," said McGrath, laughing, "why not? Might as well go all the way."

The negro in the watch cap leaned out of his machine. "Hey, mister," he said, "how'd'ja like to get that freak outta my machine?"

14

Chapter Three

———◆———

From the moment the flatbed truck delivered the wreck to the auto shop it was Dantley's car. Everyone accepted that. McGrath watched with bemused restraint while the rest of the class waited for Dantley to tell them how the car should be off-loaded, where it should be put, what should be done to it first. Of course, they made a variety of raucous sounds at him, called him a turkey, a dodo, a dummy, a klutz. But they waited, listened, and followed his suggestions. It wasn't only that he was a senior; Ricci was a senior too, and so was Kuchinsky. But Dantley unquestionably knew more about Corvettes than anyone else in the class—probably more, even, than McGrath—and he had the knack with tools and the taste for excellence that the others respected. They knew that if Dantley had his way they would take part in the rebuilding of a superb machine and, in the end, they would all get to drive it once before the school board sold it away. Only once before had McGrath seen such natural control in action.

So, while the teacher maintained an air of benign detachment, Dantley supervised every detail; he taught Kootz how to lap the valves; he patiently helped Kuchinsky to weld the frame; and he even showed Ricci how to balance the pistons. He discussed endlessly with McGrath and with anyone else who was interested the pros and cons of each new part they required. Bit by bit they all—even the thickest and the laziest—became involved in Dantley's dreams.

15

Suddenly, for Dantley, school meant Stingray. He started to arrive at eight o'clock, sometimes earlier, and he got one of the janitors to let him in so that he could work for an hour before classes started. He spent all his spares on the car, reveling every minute in the beauty of what it had once been and what it would be again. He tried any number of outlandish excuses to free himself of other classes, and when teachers finally lost patience and spoke to McGrath, the auto teacher only grinned and shrugged. "Never seen such a keen kid," he said. "What would you do if the kid was that keen for history—*discourage* him?" Sometimes Dantley even returned at night and wandered from door to door hoping that the watchman might let him in, but he never did.

"Kenny, Kenny," his mother said once on one of the rare evenings when she was home, "you're drivin' me *crazy* just sittin' around here reading car magazines. Why don't you go *out* someplace?"

"Where?"

"Well . . . movies . . . bowling . . . you never ride your bike anymore, and I paid good money . . ."

"When I was twelve."

"What?"

"You bought it when I was twelve," he said. "It was a birthday present."

"Well, it's still a good . . ."

"Hey," he said. "I'm eighteen. Notice? You expect me to ride around on a *banana seat?*"

"Oh, God. Next thing you'll want a car. I can see it coming."

He wanted to tell her about the Corvette. He had wanted to tell her for weeks, but somehow the time had never been quite right. He didn't see her often, and when he did either she was drunk or there was someone else with her. Strangely enough, as the time passed he began to enjoy his secret. He began to plan a surprise: when the car was finished and they were taking it on the field trip down to Van Nuys Boulevard, when

16

all the others had had their turns at the wheel, he would ask Mr. McGrath if he could drive it back to the school alone. Then he would bring it slowly up and around the trailer park, and he would step out of this machine, this most fabulous of cars, this coach that would make all the LTDs and Cadillacs and Skylarks that usually picked up his mother look absolutely sick, and he would stroll up and tap a knuckle on the door and say, "Hey there. Let's go for a little ride. Let's move a little."

That dream formed slowly, and he began to protect it stubbornly despite all temptations to destroy it. In October, for example, she said, "Mr. Hefferman called from the school. He says you're failing social studies. He said you don't understand even the simplest things, like"—she consulted a scribbled note—"'upward mobility'." He had almost told her then about the marvelous car taking shape under his personal supervision. He had wanted to take her shoulders and describe his vision of this car in gorgeous, technicolor detail, and explain exactly why it was that the tangible, finished form of this machine was so infinitely superior to all that porridge Heffernan tried to feed them in social studies. Instead, he just said, "I'll pass it. Don't worry."

In November, when she said, "Mr. Pingree called. You're failing physics," he had laughed incredulously, his head full of ratios, percentages, and acceleration graphs, all concerning the car and all beautifully dovetailed to the single end of maximum Corvette function; and he had come very close to telling her what in his opinion real physics was all about.

Just before Christmas she told him, "Mr. Redman called from the school. He startled me because his voice is so like your father's was. I thought for a moment . . . Anyway, he says your essay on poetry in"—and again she consulted a note—"the mid-Victorian Period . . ."

He had thought then of the Stingray moving over

17

the crest of a hill, drifting around a cambered bend, and he had said, "Mr. Redman doesn't even know what a poem is."

"Well, it's your work," she had said, waving her hands. "It's your life. I've told you that a hundred times. And God knows I've tried to raise you to be independent . . ."

"Yeah . . ."

"But I don't want any more calls from the school, Kenny. I just can't be bothered with them."

"Don't worry," he said. "I'll pass 'em all. Hardearned D's." *All but one*, he thought. In Auto Shop there would not be a D; there would be a big, beautiful, golden A.

Shortly before Christmas, work on the undercarriage was completed with the installation of a Greenwood rear suspension system—"Nothing but the best all the way," McGrath said—and they began to discuss rebuilding the shattered body. Only then did Dantley produce the clay model that he had sculpted, alone in the art room. Even in the flat gray of the modeling clay it was so sleek that it drew murmurs of admiration from the other members of the class. Impulsively and reverently they reached out to caress it—chin and rear spoilers, fenders scooping across enlarged wheel wells, discreet hood scoop.

"What's gonna be under that scoop, Ricci?" McGrath asked.

"Holly 650."

"Good. What manifold . . . Kuchinsky?"

"Hmm . . . Holley Dominator."

"Good. Mercury side-pipes?"

Dantley nodded.

"Wheels?"

"Superior Dynamo," Dantley said.

"Tires?"

"Goodrich TA's would be perfect. Eight inches on the front, ten on the rear. But . . ." He shrugged.

"It might not be impossible," McGrath said. "Leave

it to me. The first thing I'll do is get Morse Auto Parts to give us the wheels—publicity, you know. Then I'll let Dave Snelling know that. He'll give us the tires just to keep up. Wait and see." He grinned around at his class. "What it is, is blackmail."

Happily they punched and jostled one another.

"Okay," McGrath said. "Now let's build a body."

Until the end of term the sickly-sweet odor of fiberglass rose from the auto shop and permeated the school. McGrath shrugged at the complaints of teachers and administration alike. "Learning experience," he said. "Jeez, once a year at least we all get gassed by hydrogen sulphide from the chem labs. Nobody complains, right? It's a learning experience; an *academic* learning experience."

And Dantley continued his learning experience until the car was almost finished, until only the last refinements remained to be done. On the last day of the term he replaced the big steering wheel—which in his opinion was not only aesthetically offensive but also downright unnecessary, given the car's efficient power steering—with the far more attractive wheel from a Vega GT which he and Kootz had found in a scrap yard far out in the east end. And to compensate, he fitted a relief valve from a Chevy van into the steering pump. He also installed a 34-½ inch wink panel mirror to eliminate the blind spot in the right rear quarter. He fitted in the new Group 27 battery with scarcely a quarter of an inch to spare, and he replaced the stock OEM starter with an L-88 heavy-duty unit to give the modified, high-compression engine a higher cranking speed. Finally, late that afternoon, he began work on the front suspension. He began knowing that he would make these adjustments many, many times until he was perfectly satisfied, but to start he wanted 1° negative camber, a 2½° positive caster, and a ⅛ toe-in.

McGrath was right; no scholar or scientist had ever gone to work more methodically or with a more disciplined joy in his endeavor.

Early on Christmas Eve while McGrath and his wife were wrapping the last of the presents, he remembered that he had left his son's model Thunderbird in the bottom drawer of his desk at school. He drove down, let himself in, and worked his way through the darkened halls toward the shop. Somewhere in the upper levels the choir was holding its final rehearsal for the Christmas Day concert, and the sound of soft carols echoed down to him. At the Auto Shop door he paused, alert, sniffing. Drifting underneath was the unmistakable odor of fresh resin. *Damn!* Some kid had left the top off a can; either that, or worse, a can had fallen off the shelf and slopped its contents across the floor. *Great way to spend Christmas Eve, cleaning up!* He turned his key and opened the door.

The shop lay in deepening shadow except for a single wire-caged bulb hooked at the nose of the Corvette. There, crouched in the circle of light and so intent on his work that he did not notice McGrath's arrival, was Dantley.

"Hey, kid."

"Oh, hi, sir."

"What are you doing here? Who let you in?"

"Nobody. Came in the back door when they were taking the garbage out. Nobody even saw me."

"In *here*. I mean."

"Aw . . ." Grinning, Dantley produced a plastic playing card—the ace of diamonds—from his shirt pocket and flicked it off his thumbnail. "I been in here lots of times when nobody else was. Easy."

McGrath closed the door softly. He crossed to where Dantley was working, hitching up his trousers as he walked. "But what are you *doing*, kid?"

"Modifying this spoiler. It wasn't right. It just wasn't *right*, y'know, Mr. McGrath? It was this angle, here. See, the problem was . . ."

"Hey. Kid. It's Christmas *Eve*."

Dantley nodded. "Yeah."

20

"Well, the thing is that usually on Christmas Eve . . ."

"Mr. McGrath, don't tell me all that about family and stuff, okay? I know the way it's supposed to be, but it isn't like that for me. My old man's to hell and gone someplace and my mother's out working. Putting food on the table, she says. You want me to sit in the trailer by myself watchin' the dumb *tele*vision?" He turned back to the car. "Besides, this was botherin' me. It wasn't right."

Frowning, McGrath lowered himself onto a stool and for a few minutes looked closely at what the boy was doing. "That is better," he said.

"Yeah, really."

McGrath touched his fingertips together and stared down at them. "Kenny, look. Why don't you come back out to my place for a couple-three hours. We could maybe have a swim in the pool, bit of supper, afterwards I'll drive you home. No, *you'll* drive home and I'll take the car back. How's that sound?"

"Naw. Thanks, Mr. McGrath. Thanks but no thanks. You got your own kids and everything. Besides, I'm gonna be here awhile yet."

"You sure?"

"Sure."

McGrath crossed to his desk and took a half-full bottle of Cutty Sark and two glasses out of a drawer. "Well, at least you can have a drink with me, okay?" He poured.

Dantley laid down his tools and wiped his hands. "Okay. That wine?"

"Scotch."

"I had some wine once. Didn't like it much."

"Merry Christmas," McGrath said.

Dantley sniffed his glass. "Smells like my old lady most of the time," he said. "Well, here's to General Motors."

They drank in silence, both turning automatically toward the car. "That," McGrath said, "right there, is

21

going to be the most beautiful car ever to go through those doors. By far."

Dantley nodded thoughtfully. "Finished, how much do you think it'll bring?"

"Hard to tell. Auctions are funny. Remember last year's Camaro? Some slob from Palos Verdes nabbed it for $2,900. But with this one the school board should do a lot better than that."

"Yeah, but come on. How much?"

"Well, there's a lot of expensive equipment on there. A *lot* of equipment."

"More than five thousand?"

McGrath nodded slowly. "I've had the school board put $6,500 insurance on it, and the way it's going I'd say that's gonna be kinda light."

Dantley exhaled softly between his teeth, and then his jaw set. "I'm still gonna bid on it," he said.

"Isn't it a bit steep?"

"I work weekends pumping gas. And I've got a summer job lined up."

"Summer isn't that long, kid."

"My mother'll help. I know she will. As soon as she sees that car she'll help raise a down payment for it."

McGrath shook his head. "An auction means cash on the barrel head. No, don't go getting your heart set on that car, Kenny." He drank and looked at the boy, and his left eye began to tic slightly the way it did when he was very tired or very worried. He knew he had just said something foolish; he knew that Kenny Dantley's heart was set on nothing in the world *except* that car, and the knowledge troubled him deeply. His frown made large furrows down his forehead and around the corners of his mouth. "Look, kid. The car is going to go. I can guarantee you."

Dantley had scarcely touched his Scotch. He left it on McGrath's desk, walked over to the Stingray, and very slowly moved around it, looking and caressing.

"That is just a car," McGrath said behind him. "A hunk of metal and fiberglass. Believe me, Kenny, I

22

been around cars all my life, and I can tell you, you don't want to get too attached to them. They get old. They rot. They fall apart. There's something *wrong* with a man if he gets too attached to a car, know what I mean? They're just machines, after all. They're just there to be used and forgotten about."

The kid was standing in the shadows at the rear of the car, hands on his hips. His face was in shadow. "You don't fool me, Mr. McGrath. You might have seen a lot of cars, but you love this one just as much as I do."

"It's a fine machine. Sure it is. Sure I like it." McGrath poured himself another Scotch. "But I'm gonna tell you something else. I've seen a lot of cars and I've taught a lotta kids. You know I've been teaching twenty years? Twenty years, how about that! Anyway, the truth is that in all that time I only had one other student who came close to being as good as you. If you were to bring your other marks up, if you were to work hard for Forrie Redman in English, for example . . ."

Dantley grunted. He didn't like Redman; he didn't trust him.

". . . you could get a good mark if you tried. Same with all the other subjects. And then there's no telling what you could do. Junior college, maybe. Maybe even the Art Center. Why, you might end up making designs just as good as George Barris's, or Ed Roth's. You have *real ability*. You could really make something of yourself, and what I don't want is to read in the newspaper some morning a year or two from now that you've been caught holding up filling stations or knocking over milk stores to support your car habit. Take my advice, Kenny: don't try for too much too soon. That way you'll keep honest and healthy."

"There's gotta be a way," Dantley said. He came back into the light, running his hand up the flank of the car and across its roof.

"There isn't."

"People do it. Look at you, Mr. McGrath. Nice house, nice car, van . . . I don't know what a teacher makes, but . . ."

McGrath laughed quickly. His left eye began to twitch again. "There's a lot of hard work there, kid. Lotta saving. Didn't come overnight. Hey, are you gonna finish this drink?"

"Maybe later."

"Well," McGrath picked up the cellophane-sealed box containing the model Thunderbird and shook it so that the plastic pieces rattled. "This is what I came down to get. For my son. Start 'em young, eh?"

Dantley grinned and shrugged.

"I can see what I'll be doing tomorrow. Well, Merry . . . See you in January, Kenny."

"Sure thing, Mr. McGrath. Merry Christmas."

McGrath waved and started for the door. "Oh. I guess I have to give you an official reprimand for breaking in here. I'm told the school frowns on criminal activities."

"What's a reprimand?"

"Shit."

"Oh, yeah. Okay." He waved and grinned. He was already working on the spoiler again.

McGrath went out into the cool, shadowy hall and shut the door. Then he stood for a moment with his hand on the doorknob. "But the *really* important thing," he said softly to himself, "is not to get caught."

Very early on Christmas morning the lights of an approaching automobile swept over the tiny, cluttered, fenced-in backyards of the trailer park where Kenny Dantley lived, and came to rest finally on the front steps of the Dantley trailer. Kenny sat hunched on the cinder-block steps. He didn't move when the headlights found him, or when they winked out, leaving only the soft glow of the parking lights. He didn't move through the ten-minute interval which followed, or when his mother, giggling, stepped out of the passenger's door.

She was wearing one of the low-cut dresses that she wore when she worked. She leaned back through the window, said something to the driver, and then began to make her way unsteadily toward the trailer as the lights flashed back on, the engine started, and the LTD swung away.

"Why," she said. "Kenny."

"Hi. Merry Christmas."

"Why aren't you inside asleep?"

"You took the key."

"But the one in the mailbox . . . Oh!" She put a hand to her mouth. "Oh yeah. I guess I *did* take it. I guess I left my key ring . . ."

"Who was that?" Kenny raised his chin in the direction of the departing car.

"Mr. Borodino. From Southwest Land Management." She was fumbling with the lock; he stood up and took the key away from her and opened the door. "Why?"

"His water pump's going," Kenny said. "You should tell him."

Chapter Four

In the spring, two weeks before school finished, there was a hectic round of parties, culminating in the Graduation Ball. Dantley did not attend any of these events; he was never asked to parties, and the thought of inviting a girl out anywhere, let alone to a dance, terrified him. Girls laughed at him. Every girl he had ever known had laughed at him; he never quite knew why. Perhaps it was because of the way he walked— stiffly and watchfully, as if he expected to be attacked. Perhaps it was because of his left-handedness, or the sad, vacant look in his eye. Or perhaps it was simply because he himself rarely smiled, never laughed. In any case, he saw no reason why he should subject himself to the ridicule of women, whatever the reason. Some- day, he thought—and visions of the Corvette glided past his eyes—someday they would stop laughing.

On the night of the graduation dance to which he was qualified to go, having passed all subjects, he walked down alone to the school and stood watching from the shadows across the street. Music swelled through the open doors of the gym and couples drifted in and out, talking, smoking, laughing, sipping soft drinks from little paper cups. Occasionally he recog- nized someone; once he caught a glimpse of Rosa Phil- ippini, unmistakable because of the length of her hair, which had never been cut. He shrank deeper into the shadows when he saw her, because once, with some of her friends giggling in the background, she had come up to him in the hall and rubbed her breast against his arm, and when he had recoiled she had laughed and called him a faggot. That had happened in his first year of high school; he didn't even know what a faggot was.

After awhile he shrugged, kicked at a stone on the sidewalk, and, still keeping to the shadows well back from the lights of approaching cars, ambled down toward the auto shop. The side door was open. He entered and moved quickly down the corridor, taking two items from his jacket pocket as he did so. The first was a plasticized playing card—the ace of diamonds. The second was a slender glassine envelope containing a chrome casting. He slipped off the envelope and crumpled it into his pocket. Bared, the whiplash chrome letters flashed and shimmered even in the reduced light of the corridor. Dantley held the casting at arm's length and moved it smoothly, horizontally, as if it were passing on a fender under the mercury vapor lights of Van Nuys Boulevard: STINGRAY. He reversed it and turned a slow circle in the opposite direction, his lips forming the liquid sound of carburetors drawing air and of rubber on pavement: ssssshh . . . STINGRAY!

The following Monday afternoon only a very small crowd gathered outside the auto shop to witness the emergence of the Corvette. Most of these were academic students passing on their way to their own cars and distracted by the small flurry of activity, by the roar that emerged when Dantley started the engine, and by the presence of a reporter from the school newspaper, a plain, bespectacled young woman in a long skirt.

The car appeared. It was so brilliantly, deeply red that it seemed not so much to reflect the sun as to be itself a source of energy. Later, having asked McGrath the question, the reporter would be told that the illusion of actual depth in the finish had been obtained "by painting candy-apple lacquer over three pounds of gold metal flake, one-half pound of Alpha Jewels, one-quarter pound of crushed mirror, finished with five gallons of clear, rubbed out, sanded, and waxed with Meguiar's M-I," a description which left her with a slightly glazed expression. "Very shiny," she wrote. "Very, very shiny."

The four rectangular headlights were set far back into the hood and fenders, and between them protruded a sleek, sharp nose. Underneath, set into a spoiler that swept down to only a few inches above the pavement, were the oversized parking lights, and licking rear from them, up over the wheel wells, down the flanks and off the tail, were brilliant, flamboyant, orange flames edged in white. The Mercury sidepipes linked up, under the left door, with the slender tube that was the muffler, and ended in a neat chrome elbow of an exhaust pipe just in front of the rear wheel. The hood cowling which covered the high Holley carburetor was immense, reaching up on the left side in air-scoops like four blunt hands and, on the right, tilting back in six easy stages like a toppling rank of dominoes. Two roof panels, snugly fitted, were neatly designed to lift out, individually or together. The rear was covered with a broad panel proudly bearing the name STINGRAY, and topped by an oversized chrome gas hatch. In the left rear corner trembled a filament of antenna. From front to rear the car radiated power and demanded attention.

But what startled the reporter most, when she had recovered from her initial shock, was that, when she bent down to photograph the driver on the left side, there was no one there. Instead, Dantley was on the other side, right hand in control of the tiny wheel, proud left hand resting casually on the gear shifter.

"Why *is* that?" she asked Kootz, who was closest.

"Because," Kootz said, shrugging, "it's really his, see, and that's just the way he wanted it."

When the car stopped and Dantley had emerged, she asked everyone who had helped to build the car to gather around the back of it for a final picture. She had to back up quite far, there were so many bodies crowding in, and she had to wait a full minute until all the happy jostling and punching had ceased. She took her picture, wiggled her fingers in a wave of thanks, and whined off in her Datsun to file her story. Later, when she looked at the proofs, she noticed something intriguing. Everyone in that last picture was wearing a huge grin, even the teacher—McGrail, or McPhail, or whatever his name was—everyone but the slim, alert, wary kid who had driven the machine out of the shop. Beneath the peaked brim of his cap his eyes were very serious, and he was not smiling. He was looking at the camera as if he wanted to speak to it, tell it something, and he was touching, very lightly with the fingers of his left hand, the whiplash letters across the tail: STINGRAY.

After the reporter had left, a two-vehicle procession organized at the rear of the school and slowly wound up the ramp and into the street. Leading the way was McGrath's van. McGrath drove, clutching his CB mike. In the back, crowded around the rear windows, was the entire Auto Shop class, except for Dantley and Kootz. The Corvette followed with Dantley at the wheel and Kootz, also clutching a mike, perched on the passenger's seat to his left, eyes glazed in ecstasy. The machine moved with feline ease, perfect to the last bolt. Dantley knew it was perfect without checking any of the gauges (although he checked the gauges constantly), or without having to ask anyone any questions (although he did ask questions).

"Kootz, did you torque the exhaust manifold?"

"Yeah," said Kootz. "Sure. Just like you told me. Why?"

"Just thought I heard a chirp, that's all."

"I did it, Kenny. Honest. "Forty foot-pounds."

"Fifty-five." McGrath's voice crackled loud and clear through the CB. "Remember that that's the speed limit, Dantley, and stay behind me!"

"Yessir," Kootz said. "We will."

Dantley lifted his hands from the wheel. The

machine tracked straight as an arrow on the flat pavement of the freeway. He adjusted the mirror. He checked the gauges. He asked, "Did you align the lights?", although he knew that Kootz had aligned the lights with great care and precision.

There he was, behind the wheel of his Corvette. In control. He felt absolutely at home and at ease—well perhaps not *completely* at ease, for he felt a trembling excitement that began in the pit of his stomach and worked its way down into his thighs and up into the slim muscles of his chest. He revealed nothing. Only he knew it was there; it was not fear, not the terrible, cold, convulsive thing he felt with girls; it was more an eagerness, an anticipation. What he was anticipating, as the climax of the evening, was to take the car home.

He had not asked McGrath's permission yet, but he knew exactly when he would ask. He would wait until the last student had taken his turn behind the wheel and had radioed that he was returning; then, in the few moments before the Corvette glided up behind Mc-Grath's van for the trip home, Dantley would ask. He would tell McGrath completely honestly what he wanted to do, and McGrath would say, "Yeah, sure, kid. Go ahead. Just be sure to meet me back at the school at ten so we can lock it up for the night, okay?" Then he would step down into the car and pull smoothly out into the traffic, and McGrath would tell the others, "Little treat for standing at the top of the class. Wants to take his girl for a ride . . ."

"Hey." Kootz's voice tugged Dantley out of his reverie. "Look what pulled up beside us. Hey! Wow!"

Dantley looked to see that another car had drawn even with them and was moving precisely abreast, two lanes over. Swiftly he assessed it: '57 Chevy Bel Air. Crimson. Tail jacked up provocatively. Double pumper Holley. Driver looking across at Dantley and at the Stingray as if they were something left by a sick dog.

"Neat!" said Kootz.

Dantley swung on him. "Whatya mean, *neat!* Jeez,

30

Kootz, you know what that is? It's a can, that's all! A heap!" He touched the gear shift. He glanced into his mirrors and noted that the lane between him and the Chevy was clear. He looked across again at the other driver and saw that he was grinning—grinning and saying something. Dantley read his lips: *Gutless.*

"Don't do it!" Again McGrath's voice crackled over the CB. "Don't even *think* about it, Dantley!" But in the background Dantley could hear the others shouting, "Do it! Do it! Stomp it! Suck the doors off that vacuum cleaner!" And he looked up at the eager, encouraging faces and waving fists in the van's rear windows.

"Dantley, I'm warning you . . ."

"Turn it off, Kootz," he said. In the same instant, in one smooth movement, he swung into the center lane and floored the accelerator.

"Oh," said Kootz, crunching down into his seat and holding on. "Oh, *shit!*"

Smoke poured from the big rear treads, and the Corvette lunged with such power that it seemed to those watching in McGrath's van that it would be airborne before it passed them. In a second it had flashed past, the Chevy straining beside it, both exhausts roaring like jets. "Go, Kenny! Go! Go!" Kuchinsky was screaming with excitement and pounding the back of McGrath's seat.

"You got him!" Ricci said.

"Rotten kid!" McGrath said, but he was smiling.

Behind the wheel of the Corvette, Dantley was in a kind of euphoric trance. He was aware simultaneously of the crimson shape striving to keep abreast of him on the far side of Kootz's cowering form, and of cars flashing past on his right, and of the perfect functioning of every part of the Stingray. For the very first time in his life he was confident, completely confident, of winning. He was in control. He and the machine were one. Time ceased to exist, sounds dropped away. He flew.

Afterward, when Kootz told him that the race had only lasted about four minutes, maybe five, Dantley couldn't believe it. It seemed much longer. It seemed like a glorious lifetime during which the world and all that was in it existed for him alone. Looking back, he could not separate any one incident from the others until, near the end, the freeway traffic thinned out suddenly and the cleared, flat road stretched as far as he could see. He glanced at the Chevy beside him, smiled (at least Kootz said he smiled; Dantley couldn't remember), and pressed his foot down, down, down, until it could go no farther. He knew everything that was happening inside the massive engine, but even so, the amount of power remaining astonished him. The car responded instantly, all the way to the floor, and it moved away from the Chevy as effortlessly as if the other car had been standing still. The other driver tried his best—Kootz said he looked like a weight-lifter, eyes bulging and neck tendons standing out—and for a few minutes the Chevy actually kept up the pace. But then its overworked transmission gave up. With a terrible grinding of expensive parts, transmission oil smoking as it spattered on the hot exhaust, the Chevy swerved, slowed, hit the shoulder, and came to a fuming, jolting stop.

Dantley swung up onto the next cloverleaf and back down into the return lane of the freeway. He drove at a decorous fifty-five, the engine humming comfortably. By the time he reached the still-smoking Chevy, a cruiser had pulled in behind it, and an officer with his cap on the back of his head was saying something to the disconsolate driver about the smoke and the half-mile of strewn metal. Dantley cruised past on the other side of the median, and when he saw the other driver looking at him he waved, shrugged, and mouthed a word clearly enough to be understood across the distance: *Gutless.*

The mercury vapor lights had already come on along Van Nuys Boulevard when Dantley pulled in behind McGrath's waiting van. The kids sprawled comfortably on the roof and fenders, but spilled off when they saw the Corvette, cheering and applauding. They milled around the car, punching Dantley's shoulder and tousling his hair, and McGrath had to fight his way through to the driver's window.

"Where the hell have you been?"

"Sorry, sir. Missed the exit."

"You coulda been *killed!*" McGrath said. "You coulda been arrested!"

Kootz emerged from the passenger's seat and leaned across the roof of the car, smiling deliriously. "Hey, sir. Sir. Can I tell you about this car? Do you know what this car did? It laid rubber in fourth!"

"Horse shit!" said Ricci, after a moment of awed silence.

"No shit." Kootz shook his head soberly. "True."

"All right, all right," said McGrath. " 'Way you go, now. You each got ten minutes. Ricci, you're first. Hey, Dantley, Ricci's turn, okay? C'mon, kid, climb out. You don't *own* the car, y'know. As a matter of fact, after that little race of yours, we're lucky that *anybody* else has a chance to drive it."

After Ricci had motored out into the traffic, Dantley turned to his teacher. "That," he said, "is the finest car in the world."

"Well, I dunno about that," McGrath said, "but it's a beauty, a honey." He lowered his voice and glanced around. "Tell me, did you really leave rubber in fourth?"

"I didn't notice," Dantley said, grinning. "I wasn't thinking about what was behind me."

The boulevard that night was even more active than usual. It was warm, it was clear, it was an ideal evening to cruise, to see and be seen, to show off the custom jobs that had taken such hours of painstaking labor. On Van Nuys Boulevard, that summer night like others, the hot rod was king. Harassed police tried to check all vehicles for possible traffic violations, but it was impossible; new cars appeared by the moment bearing modifications and customized features that left the officers scratching their heads and frowning at their copies of the Motor Vehicle Code. Races developed at a dropped word or a disdainful glance, like mushrooms springing up on a damp night, and the entire boulevard turned into a pulsating, throbbing, raucous, fume-laced carnival of posturing and automotive display.

One by one the members of McGrath's class took their turns guiding the Corvette out into this metallic river, and one by one, if only for the meager ten minutes that McGrath allowed them, they felt the thrill of being accepted into that river which, to them, was the stream of life itself. For those minutes they commanded the power that caught the attention and respect of their peers. For ten minutes it didn't matter how skinny they were, or how fat, or how much they smelled, or who their parents were, or if they were hopelessly stupid, or if they were dismally cursed to a lifetime of boils, acne, pimples, chancres, hives, and other eruptions. For ten minutes, the ten minutes that symbolized their part in making it a thing of beauty, they got to drive The Car. And then heads turned, horns tooted admiringly, and whistles floated toward them in the sultry California evening.

One after another, the class experienced this transcending pleasure. The only condition was that they must use the CB to report their positions every few minutes. So, for two hours, the class sprawled on the roof of McGrath's van or lounged against its fenders, well within range of the CB speaker, either anticipating their own drive or experiencing it electronically, vicariously, once again. "Five minutes," McGrath would say. "Make your turn now." But it always took a minute longer, just to find the spot to turn; and then, of course, the return trip was always made as slowly as possible, so that most of the solo flights took closer to fifteen minutes than to ten, and by the time everyone else had had a turn and only Kootz remained, it was after eleven, and McGrath looked very tired and very tense.

Jeez, looks about eighty-five, thought Dantley, watching him, seeing how the street lights thickened the pockets under his eyes and deepened the furrows around his mouth. He had never seen McGrath actually look *ugly* before, and he was beginning to worry about asking his favor, especially after the incident with the crimson Chevy, when McGrath turned to him and chuckled.

"Why so worried, kid? Oh, I get it. Think I'm still ticked off about the little drag race, eh? Well, forget it. I'm not. To tell you the truth, I would've done the same thing myself." He called over to the parked Corvette. "All right, Kootz. Ten minutes. Then we all go home." He glanced at his watch.

Proudly, nervously, Kootz climbed behind the wheel, waved the others away from the fenders, shifted neatly into first, and stalled.

"Klutz," Ricci said.

"Yeah—it's this damn clutch!" Kootz shouted.

"If it's too much for you, Kootz," Kuchinsky said in her very best Mae West voice, "just give me a call."

Everyone laughed but Dantley. "Take your time," he said, and then held his breath until Kootz had negotiated away from the curb, around the van, and out into traffic. "He'll be okay," he said to McGrath, and noticed as he did so that the teacher was nervous too; his forehead and upper lip were filmed with sweat. *Not now,* Dantley thought. *I'll ask when Kootz is on the way back, when he's almost here.*

But almost immediately after Kootz had turned around, at the far end of his run, McGrath was squeezing the CB mike. "Kootz, where are you? How far up the road didja get? You don't have to come back yet, why didja turn around so soon?"

"Just saw a place, Mr. McGrath. And a girl." The Stingray's horn beeped.

"How far are you from Bob's?"

35

"Bob's? About half a block. I see it dead ahead."

"Tell you what, let's celebrate with a round of Cokes. Park on the side street out of traffic and run in there. I want eight large Cokes and a Sprite for me. Got that?"

"Roger. Wilco. Ten four. Over and out."

McGrath shook his head. "Steve McQueen," he said. Then, into the mike: "Kootz: *Take the keys!* Lock it up and take the keys! Jeez," he added, his left eye twitching, smiling queerly at Dantley, "I hope he remembers."

Ten minutes later there was no sign of Kootz. In fifteen minutes he still had not appeared. McGrath's calls into the CB brought only static. McGrath was sweating heavily now, and dark half-moon stains under his armpits had begun to spread down his shirt. As for Dantley, fear began to twist like a wakening snake in his belly. After twenty minutes, McGrath waved them into the van. "Let's go," he said. "We'll find him."

They did. Kootz was staggering up the sidewalk like a bomb victim, his pathetically frail arms spread with shock. When he saw the van he stopped, and when Dantley sprang out and seized him, shaking him, shouting, "Where is it? *Where's the car?*" He began to cry.

"You lost it! Jesus, you *lost* it!"

"I couldn't help it. It wasn't my fault! I locked it, just like Mr. McGrath said. Honest to God I did, I *locked* it! Whoever took it must've had a *key!*"

Dantley pushed him away. For a moment he stared at Kootz's pathetic, dirty, streaky face. He wanted to scream and curse. Never had he envied people with words as much as he did at that moment. But he could say nothing, nothing at all. Instead, the dread that had been seething in his gut for the previous half hour suddenly burst out of him and turned to engulf him—a huge, soft, infinitely expanding red flower of rage that fluttered maddening petals across his eyes, and in his armpits and groin and palms, causing him to utter one

36

terrible scream of rage and to lunge at the throat of the hapless Kootz. Before the others had pulled him off, Kootz's face had turned deep red and he was making sounds like a snorkler in surf. Dantley had found his voice: "You . . . dumb . . . schmuck . . ." He shook free and reeled a few paces down the street bent over, gasping, elbows on knees, as if he had run a long long way. Then he shook his fist in the air—at McGrath, at the class, and at the whole rotten city behind them. "I'll find it," he said. "You watch!" In the back of his mind, infuriatingly, was the one detail that he had intended to add but had forgotten—a solenoid valve in the fuel line, connected to a toggle switch would have foiled the theft.

"The police . . ." McGrath began.

"Fuck the police! *I'll* do it." He hit his chest. "Me." Then he turned and began to jog away from them down the sidewalk, picking up speed as he went.

The Sheriff's Deputy came to the school mainly because Ernie Bacon, the principal, thought his talk would be a good learning experience: "What *good* can come of this, Ed?" he asked, when McGrath told him of the theft. "After all, every cloud . . ." He was always encouraging his staff to think positively, to look on the sunny side, to turn every misfortune into a triumph, and so on.

So the Sheriff's Deputy came, and Mr. Bacon, looking very serious, took a back stool in the auto shop. The Sheriff's Deputy was out of shape and sweated a lot. He wore thick shoes. He had brought a slide show which, he told Mr. McGrath, he would run through for the boys if there was time after his talk. It showed, he said, the perils of drinking and driving. His name was Wychowsky and he was in public relations; he certainly did not project the same image of the Los Angeles Police Department that Dantley and the others had formed from watching many hours of television. He heaved himself onto a stool and spoke straight from the shoulder. "Slim," he said. "That's what your, our chances of finding that car are. And getting slimmer every day. Why? I'll tell you why, boys . . ."

"Boys and *girl*, goddammit!" Kuchinsky shouted.

"Sorry, Miss . . ."

"Ms."

"Mzz. Well, the reason why we're not likely to find your car is that there is one car stolen in the greater Los Angeles area *every seven minutes!* We're a good police force, among the best in the country, but nobody, *nobody* can keep on top of that kind of theft. So after five days we usually tell an owner—being candid, you understand—to consider his car gone for good. A write-off."

"Like my Toronado," said Mr. Bacon ruefully.

"Right on," said Sergeant Wychowsky, and someone at the back of the room groaned audibly. "The fact is that there are a number of theft rings operating in this town. There's likely one right in this neighborhood. And they are very smooth, very sophisticated. They have keys, faked papers, inside information. And what they will do when they make a hit is take that car right across state lines, probably the same night, and they will cut it up."

"No!" Dantley suddenly came to life after half-listening, head down on his desk, exhausted and discouraged after two days of fruitless search. He surprised even himself that he had energy left to leap out of his seat at the image of the Stingray inert and helpless in some grubby garage, at the mercy of ruthless chopsaws. Both fists hit the desk. "Like hell anybody'll cut that car up!"

"Know how you feel, son," Wychowsky said, "but the fact is . . ."

"The fact is that we're talking about a car that's absolutely one of a kind. It's unique. Unmistakable. You've *got* the description, for crissake! The instant that car's driven, if you guys were doing your job, it should be spotted and picked up."

Wychowsky nodded tolerantly. "It's not that easy, uh . . . uh . . ."—he consulted the seating plan McGrath had thoughtfully provided—". . . Kenny. See, they'll use a transport."

"Transport?"

"Sure. Semi. Nobody'd be stupid enough to *drive* that car out of here on any major highway. So, they just slide it into a nice roomy tractor trailer and seal it up. Open only at destination." He spread his hands. "Seriously now, son, what do you really expect us to do about that kind of M.O.? Do you have any *idea* how many semis move in and out of this town in a day."

"Roadblocks," Dantley said. "Spot checks."

Wychosky shook his head. "Nope. We just simply do not have the manpower. The fact is we've just got to let most of 'em go. Insurance has gotta pick up the tab . . . What's that, Kenny?"

"I said I don't care about the insurance, or the school board, or the Los Angeles Police Department. I'm gonna find that car, and nobody's gonna cut it up. Nobody!" And with a final pounding of the desk, Dantley spun on his heel and strode from the classroom, into the bright sun on the parking lot.

"Well," said Sergeant Wychowsky after a minute, "if there are no questions, maybe we have time for the slide show?"

Chapter Five

The following day, Dantley began his summer job at the filling station. Fortunately, it was on a major throughway. He had bought ten of the papers that carried the photograph of the car, and he kept them in a box under his bed where he knew his mother would not find them. She rarely cleaned, and she certainly never looked under his bed. Besides, she did not read papers. When he began to work at the station, he clipped the pictures and scotch-taped them at eye level wherever they might be seen—on all four pumps, on the door, above the cash register, in the men's and ladies' rooms, and even in the work bays—with the question underneath: *Have You Seen This Car?* After a few days the clippings on the pumps had turned yellow and got crumpled and torn in the wind and rain, and so he went down to the newspaper office and paid them to make four big glossy prints from the negative. He covered these with plexiglass before taping them up. He watched to see if drivers and passengers noticed the pictures as their cars were being filled; if they didn't, he asked. For a while he got only shrugs, shakes of the head, and indifference.

One afternoon late in June, an aging Cadillac convertible rolled up to the pumps. The jowly, beery driver pulled from the trunk a small case that said *Carroll & Company: Health and Beauty Aids*, and winking at Dantley, went inside the men's washroom to fill up the cologne dispenser and the condom dispenser, and to toss deodorant disks into the urinals. He came out frowning, thoughtfully replaced the case and closed the trunk; then he snapped his fingers. "Yeah!" he said. "I have!" He pointed at the glassy print taped to the pump. "Damn right I've seen it."

Dantley spun away from the other car he had begun to service and moved like a tap-dancer through the racks of cans and bottles on the island. "Where? Where?"

"Vegas," the man said.

"You sure it's that car?"

He peered more closely at the print. He pointed. "What color's this?"

"Red."

"This?"

"Orange."

"Yup. It's the same machine. I'd swear on it. I tell ya, that car is in Vegas. They got it at one of the big hotels there, y'know? On a mirror. Goin' 'round and 'round."

"Which hotel?"

"Yeah, which one?" The salesman rubbed his bald head. "I was out with a client, y'know"—he winked again—"on the Strip. Truth is, I can't remember. But one of the big ones." He eased himself behind the wheel of the Cadillac and started the engine. "Right on the Strip. Can't miss it," he said, and was gone.

After work that night Dantley returned to the trailer, packed a few things in the old Marine knapsack that had been his father's, and left a note on the kitchen table for his mother. "Taking a holiday in Las Vegas," it said. "Will make my fortune ha ha. Love Kenny." He almost added "dont worry," but what the hell, why bother?

He phoned Ricci.

"Jeez," Ricci said. "It's a bad night. Aren't you goin' to graduation?"

"No."

"Well, okay. I'll run you out as far as the Colton

41

Intersection. You should be able to get a ride from there, easy."

And so they rode out that evening in Ricci's Datsun pickup—Ricci and his girlfriend in the cab, Dantley, Kuchinsky, and Kootz sprawled in the box. "Insurance paid off," Ricci shouted back through the glassless window. "McGrath says the shop's *really* set for next year. Six and a half grand, wow!"

"Yeah, yeah," said Kootz. "And we've already decided what to buy. We're gonna buy a Valiant. Nobody steals a Valiant."

Dantley regarded him for several moments before he spoke, his head tipped back against the rim of the box and his eyes half-closed. Then he said, "Kootz, you are a pathetic creep."

"Jeep," shouted Kootz. Yeah! Maybe we'll get a jeep."

"So," Ricci continued through the window, one eye on the road, "I don't know why you're doing this. I really don't. Who's suffered? I mean, really. We got the experience, the school got it's money. Everybody's a winner, right?"

"Wrong," Dantley said. "I lost."

"Well, if you ask me, it's not worth burning your ass off in the desert."

"For sure," said his girlfriend.

"My advice is to forget it," Ricci said. "What the hell, like McGrath says, it's only a chunk of metal."

"I appreciate your advice," Dantley said, looking out under the brim of his cap at the passing traffic.

"For sure," said the girl.

When they reached the Colton Intersection, Ricci stopped on the shoulder and Dantley swung out of the box, pulling his knapsack behind him. The western sky was filled with a sunset made glorious by the smog of Los Angeles; to the east, a broken stream of traffic swept toward San Bernardino and the hot, indigo sky above the Mojave desert. "Thanks for the lift," he said.

"Yeah. Take care," said Ricci.

"For sure," said the girl.

"Hey," said Kootz, digging into his pocket, "take this and play a slot for me, will ya?" He flipped Dantley a quarter.

"Sure," Dantley said. "What the hell."

Kuchinsky, who sat huddled in a corner of the truck throughout the journey, wiggled across the floor of the box on her knees, took his face in her hands, and kissed him on the forehead. She was crying. "See you," she said. "Look after yourself." And the truck pulled away and left him.

He walked awhile without trying to hitchhike. Then he turned around and stuck out his thumb. His first ride was with an old rancher who said absolutely nothing and took him as far as El Cajon. They arrived in the dark. Dantley tried hitchhiking, but it was hopeless; the few vehicles that passed were traveling well over eighty, taking advantage of the empty road, and there was no chance of their stopping for some skinny kid with a Marine knapsack and a crayoned *Las Vegas* sign. So he walked; and he was still walking when the sun came up on the empty highway. As far as he could see in both directions nothing moved—nothing but the shimmering pools of morning heat, already rising slowly from the asphalt.

It was very quiet. In the far distance a strange bird croaked, but nearby the only sound was a high-pitched humming, which could have been the baking of the sand, or the sluggish subterranean movement of desert creatures, or just the coursing of Dantley's own blood through his ears.

He was tired, hot, and beginning to get nervous. People died in places like this. People died without water, and he had no water. He began to stuff his cap into his pack, but then changed his mind and pulled it back on; he remembered a day when he was very small. He and his mother had taken the bus to the beach and she had told him to be sure to keep his hat on or else he'd get sunstroke. He had no idea what

43

sunstroke was, but he thought it must be like what he was feeling now—sort of light and dizzy. He sat on his pack and pulled his collar up. He had no idea how long he remained there—time vanished, evaporating into the high-pitched song of the sand. He sat, and listened, and watched the fluid patterns of heat melding and shifting on the highway.

Then, emerging so gradually from these liquid patterns that he could not be sure when he first actually *saw* them, there appeared several very low, shimmering shapes. He blinked and counted: five, identically colored, in a convoy so close together that they seemed in the distance to merge, and separate, and blend again, as if they had been filmed through a shaded lens with old, defective film. But the sound was unmistakable; they were unquestionably hot rods, driven by fine engines perfectly tuned. As if in a dream, Dantley stood up and extended his thumb.

Elegantly they came, so elegantly that Dantley would have been happy just to have had the pleasure of seeing them, even if they had passed him. But they did not pass. The lead car glided off the road and onto the shoulder beside him. With a slow, soothing hiss the passenger door opened to receive him, not outward and forward as in a conventional car, not upward, as in the gull-winged Mercedes that Dantley had seen photographs of once, long ago, but *downward*, drooping as gracefully as a ballerina's arm until it rested on a protective rubber pad. Dantley moved toward the car like a man in a dream, already hearing strains of langorous music, already feeling the blissful touch of cool air.

"Vegas, man?" The driver was a grinning, stocking-capped Mexican in his early twenties. He was motioning Dantley inside, down over the extended wing and in. Dantley obliged. He found himself in one of the most comfortable seats he had ever experienced. It was like a deep-foam dentist's chair. "We can take you all the way," the driver said. The door hissed closed and locked into place with the comfortable *chunk* of solid,

44

well-oiled machinery. "Here you go, man. You look as if you could use this." From somewhere beside his seat the driver produced a bottle of ice-cold ginger beer and passed it to Dantley.

"Thanks." He stared around at the furnishings as he drank. Beyond any doubt, it was one of the most resplendent cars he had ever been in. The steering wheel was chrome-plated chain-link, and very, very small. The entire dashboard was warmly irridescent. The headliner floated softly in purple angel hair. The floor was covered with an indigo shag rug of incredible loft. The leather padding on doors, dash, and ceiling was backed by what appeared to be many inches of foam. "Neat," he said respectfully. "Very neat." And yet, something was wrong. He could not quite put his finger on it, but there was definitely something wrong.

"Tico's the name," said the driver, offering his hand.

"Kenny."

"Kenny, you are obviously into cars."

"Yeah."

"Lemme guess, now." Tico glanced at him, still grinning happily. "You are clearly Anglo, right? I mean, sorry, but that's just the way it is. You . . . are . . . an . . . Anglo. So you will like some of those big Anglo cars, like . . ." He snapped his fingers. "Like Charger, or Camaro, or T-bird, or . . . or Corvette!"

"Got me," Dantley said.

"Sure I got you. Anglo, Corvette . . . Corvette, Anglo."

"Fine car, Corvette," Dantley said, warily.

"Well, sure, in some ways"—Tico looked pained—"but they are so *heavy*. I mean, they are so *powerful* and so *fast!* I mean, as far as I am concerned, you understand, they are the ultimate gross-out buggy."

At that moment Dantley realized what was wrong: they were barely moving. Semis had been sweeping past them, air horns blaring. He leaned over and glanced at the speedometer: fifteen miles an hour. He looked behind: The four other low-slung Chevies were following in a sedate line, each containing, as far as Dantley could see, only the driver. "Excuse me," he said, "but what are you doing—looking for a contact lens?"

Tico continued to smile broadly. "You see, we have a theory about you Anglo folks. It is that speed is your ultimate weapon. Since we ourselves are peace-loving, we have eschewed speed and gone very heavily into *class*, as you can see."

Another air horn bellowed, and Dantley looked around to see a purple-black, metal-flaked Kenworth cabover descending on them like a rabid dinosaur, glass eyes bulging and chrome teeth bared. Behind the wheel he glimpsed a gnomelike driver, gesticulating wildly. Terrified, he pushed back hard into his seat, expecting the next instant to be part of an accordion of Chevrolets. But somehow, by a splendid bit of driving, the trucker managed to keep control of his rig and to miss them. He swept past like a tornado, air horn blasting. Across his tailgate was a huge sticker in fluorescent letters: TRUCKERS DO IT BEST.

Tico shook his head slowly "Diesel demon. K-Whooper. 600-inch Detroit. Not cool. Not cool at all."

"Yeah, well look," Dantley said, still shaking, "I gotta get out now."

"Oh *no*, man, you can't do that!" Tico seemed genuinely concerned. "We gonna take you all the way to *Los Huevos*, remember?"

"How do you . . ."

"You can't get out, man. There's no handle. All electronic. From here." He tapped a parabolic control panel beside the steering column. "Seriously, man, you *can't* leave. What we gonna do when we get there . . ."

"The way you're going, sometime in October, right?"

"Time, man, time. What is time?" Tico opened his hands expansively. "Time is nothing. The point is that we will arrive in Las Vegas with *class*. That is every-

46

thing. And when we get there we gonna visit my aunt. She got a restaurant—The Golden Enchilada—in the suburbs. Aw, man, you *gotta* come with us; she makes the best tacos, tostadas . . . And she is *cool*, you know? She's got class, my aunt. Why, sometimes you can sit there, wait an hour, maybe two for *one taco*. With my aunt you learn it: *Time is not important!*"

"Not to you, maybe, but it is to me. I got things to do. Really. Thanks, Tico, but I got ta get out. Look, tell you what, you don't even have to stop, okay? Just lay down the door and I'll jump."

Tico shook his head regretfully as he pulled onto the shoulder and the door hissed down. "I'm really sorry about this, man. But you remember the name of my aunt's restaurant, you hear? Golden Enchilada. And if you ever need friends in Vegas you call there and ask for us: The Grenadiers. Okay?"

Dantley stepped into the heat. "Thanks," he said. "See you."

"And remember"—Tico formed a neat circle with his thumb and a middle finger—"class counts."

The door hissed up and nestled into place. Then to Dantley's astonishment the whole car began to shudder, then to bob and weave gently, and then suddenly it sprang into the air like a huge flea and hopped onto the road, followed at twenty-foot intervals by the four other Chevies. They moved as if chained together, and as each driver came abreast of Dantley he made the A-okay circle sign with thumb and finger, hit his lifts, and sent his machine wobbling, like Tico's, up on mechanized stilts. Dantley watched this weird procession totter off into the distance until it merged with the mirages out of which it had come, sometimes made tiny, sometimes magnified and distorted until it seemed like a group of stalking monsters.

"Another hallucination, goddammit!" The voice boomed out, raucous and close. There, shimmering in the heat, was a middle-aged person, now fat, now thin. He was wearing a double-knit plaid business suit, a tie,

47

and a child's hat many sizes too small for him, obviously blown out of some station wagon. "Been havin' 'em all day," he shouted hoarsely. "Hallucinations. Thought you were another one. Well, c'mon." He swung his arm. "Let's walk." And he started plodding resolutely toward Los Angeles.

Dantley got up and dusted himself off. "I'm headed *that* way."

"What! Las Vegas? Are you crazy, boy?" The man came hobbling toward him across the highway. He stopped a few feet away, crouched like a crab, and stared incredulously. "Why in God's name would you want to go *there*, my son? It is a bad, bad place which does terrible things to people. Take my advice and have no truck with it at all. Look what it did to me— all my money, gone! My car, gone! Why, I can't even afford a *bus* ticket!"

"Sorry," Dantley said. "Thing is, I've got nothing to lose."

"Ah, so you may think, young man, so you might think. But that city will take your health! It will take your sanity! Finally, it will take what you love most in all the world and debase it before your eyes. It will make a whore of it; and then, it will make a whore of *you!*"

"Very heavy," said Dantley. He picked up his bag.

"No, no, come, my son." The man plucked at his arm. "Walk with me back to Los Angeles where the air, foul though it is, is infinitely better than the poisonous stuff of Vegas."

"Sorry," Dantley said, starting to walk again. He thought that he had glimpsed a shimmering truck shape in the distance to the west, and he wanted to dissociate himself from this person before it approached. He walked fast. The man hobbled after him for only a few paces before giving up and lifting a hand in farewell. "You'll see. You'll go there a young man, full of the vigor and promise of manhood, and you'll come

48

away a broken wreck, without future, without pride, without hope. You'll see."

Dantley glanced behind. Yes, there was a truck, coming fast. He turned around again and kept walking. He wanted to put much distance between himself and this raving maniac who was, Dantley had concluded, a religious freak. In fact, at that moment he was shouting to some celestial audience. "There he goes! Another pure young soul on his way to perdition!"

The truck was actually a van, an extraordinary van, traveling much faster than Dantley had thought. All at once it was there beside, him, stopping despite the fact that he had not even had time to extend his thumb. The first thing he noticed was its superb paint job. Crimson had been laid on basic white, and maroon had been laid on the crimson in complicated and pleasing horizontal patterns designed to reinforce the illusion of length. Delicate tracery—white on red, maroon on white—trailed gracefully down the entire body. On the central panel was a flamboyant, golden name—VANESSA—and underneath was a tiny painting of two cherries on a single stem. The whole van was deeply, lovingly, lacquered and polished.

The next thing he noticed was that the driver was a girl, dark-eyed and bare-shouldered, her black hair falling forward as she reached across to open the door. He was struck by an incredible burst of sound—"That's the Way I Like It"—at least 120 decibels. "Hop in," she shouted. "Let's go."

"Perdition! Perdition!" screamed the ruined gambler, hobbling toward the van, waving both arms.

Dantley hopped—into the sound, into the blissful coolness, into a huge, swiveled armchair of sinful, gorgeous comfort. He slammed the door, leaned back, and actually shut his eyes. "Thanks. "He sighed. "Thanks of lot."

The throbbing music ceased with a click. "You're welcome. But I wasn't even sure for a minute you were hitchhiking. Listen, if you're hitchhiking you gotta stick something out, know what I mean?" she laughed.

He looked at her more closely. She was about his age, or perhaps a bit younger. It was hard to tell, because she was wearing lipstick and her eyes looked much older than the rest of her face. They were wary, like Dantley's own; and there was something else: *Never apologize,* they said. Her hair, like her eyes, was very black; large golden earrings dangled amidst its strands. She was wearing jeans and a tank top, on the chest of which was the same little two-cherry logo that appeared on the flank of her van. No brassiere. The lacquer on her fingernails matched the deepest red on her van. He noticed, for some reason, that her shoulders were freckled.

"Vegas?" she asked. Her voice was a little hoarse, as if she had mild laryngitis.

Dantley nodded. They had been accelerating rapidly and were now going at least eighty-five.

"You a gambler?"

"Not me."

"Where you from?"

"Newhall."

"Yeah? MacArthur High?"

"Just graduated," Dantley said. "Well, sort of. The thing is, I haven't actually picked up my diploma."

"I know a lot of guys from MacArthur, but I went to San Fernando. Why you going to Vegas?"

"Somebody stole my Stingray and I heard it was there. I'm going to get it."

"Stingray, wow! You got a Corvette?"

"Sure," Dantley said. "Well, sort of. The thing is . . ."

"I *love* Stingrays!"

"Yeah?"

"Sure. I think they're the sexiest damn cars!" She slapped her steering wheel. "What year?"

" 'Seventy-three."

"Aw, too bad. They really tamed that engine."

"Well, it's not stock. I put a little work on it." He thought of the car, glancing at her out of the corner of his eye. He thought of riding up effortlessly behind her van, and of overtaking and then using his right-turn signal just once and sliding in front of her and moving away. He thought of her saying to herself, "Wow, look at that car *move!*" But inside the Corvette there would be a little soft music, and Kenny Dantley cruising one-hand, alone with his thoughts. "Neat," he said.

"You like?" She grinned. "You haven't even seen the best part—go back and have a look."

He swiveled in the captain's chair and followed the broadloom through a swaying bead curtain, down a low step, and into a crushed-velvet boudoir. "Light," she said, and turned a rheostat on the dash. Gently, the swag lamps brightened, sending their reflections off the gold-shot mirrors on the ceiling, down over the plush walls and the queen-size waterbed with its leopard-skin cover. "Need more?" She turned another rheostat and around the tops of the walls tiny accent lamps winked on, filling the mirrors with starlike dots. Dantley whistled softly.

"The fridge is right beside the bed," she said. "Bring me a cold one and help yourself." He found the handle in the thick shag covering, opened the little fridge which served also as a night table, and took out two Coors. He went back through the beaded curtains and into the cab just in time to see the snaillike caravan of low riders as Vanessa swung out to pass them. "Elegance freaks," she said, shrugging. "Might as well be lawn tractors."

Dantley took a long, cool pull at his beer. "That's beautiful back there," he said. "It really is."

"Like it?" She switched off the lamps.

"Really. Lot of money there. Who did the work?"

"Friends of mine," she said. "Hell, I couldn't *afford* a setup like that; they did it for services rendered."

Dantley grinned vacantly and tipped up his beer can again.

51

The girl laughed. "On the bed. It's called the barter system. No money changes hands, just goods and services." She shrugged, drank, and licked the froth off her upper lip. "That's gonna change now, though. I'm going professional."

"Professional?"

"Hooker, dummy."

"But . . . why?"

"Well, for one thing, my old man threw me out. See, he's a Baptist and his idea of fun and mine aren't quite the same. So, when I told him that I was a barter-system hooker . . . Yeah, well, I had to tell him, eh? Just a matter of simple honesty. I couldn't go on letting him think that this van and everything in it came because *God* loved me, after all. Anyway, when I told him, he got very excited the way they do in church sometimes. He kinda frothed at the mouth and said I was a shame and a disgrace to his name, and if my mother had been alive it would have broken her heart, and so on. I told him I couldn't see what all the fuss was about; after all, the Bible says that we're supposed to love one another and bring joy into the world and so on. And that's what I'd been doing, right? I mean"—she patted the steering wheel for emphasis—"that's what I had *really been doing!* Anyway, he called me a hussy and a fallen woman and other names that nobody's used since the *ark*, for godsake, and then he told me to get out of his sight. So I did."

Dantley gaped at her as she spoke; he had never heard anyone talk so much, at least not to him. Furthermore, she wasn't laughing at him.

"Know what's gonna happen?" She pointed at him and he shook his head. "What's gonna happen is that after awhile he'll write me a please-come-home-all-is-forgiven letter. And I'll write back and I'll tell him no, no"—she flung the back of her wrist across her forehead—"that since he drove me into the streets I feel debased, tarnished, *soiled*, and unworthy to return to my father's house." She laughed and shrugged. "Aw,

52

what the hell. No I won't. I'll probably go back and see him. I love the silly old bugger."

Dantley found his voice. "So, why Vegas?"

"Why *Vegas!* Are you *ser*ious? Because if you're gonna get started in the life, Vegas is the place to be, that's all. Why, there are more hookers per capita in that town than anywhere else. Professionals and amateurs both, I mean. It's the working-girl's heaven. Some girls in Vegas, they clear a grand a week. Easy. On weekends! But you gotta have a wrinkle, know what I mean? And mine's right here: Vanessa's van—waterbed, mobility, and solid entertainment. The truth is, this really isn't a van at all, right? It's a a a rolling massage parlor, contact sport, nude-encounter, money machine." She spread her hands, stuck her tongue out, and made a deliriously happy gaga sound. And then she began to laugh. Her laughter reminded Dantley of the cranking mechanism on a big sprocket wrench.

Astonishingly, it was contagious. He began to laugh too. He had no idea how long it had been since something, or someone, had caused him to laugh, *really* to laugh. Probably years—he couldn't remember. All he knew was that something long pent-up released itself, and the sensation was marvelous. His laughter was amazingly like hers—an incredulous, scratchy, high-pitched monotone. He laughed until the tears came and he sagged over against his knees, holding himself because his chest ached. He was not sure *why* he was laughing, but it didn't matter. He was; and with a woman.

"You know," she said, wiping away the tears, "I don't even know your name." And this was enough to set them off again, both convulsed. After a moment he managed to tell her, and they laughed again, and then she said, "You're a cute guy. Let's talk."

Soon, they had another beer, rolling at a smooth eighty past the towns of Jean and Sloan and into the dusk, and Dantley swung the chair gently to and fro, rocking to the rhythms of some slow, solid music on

53

the tape deck. And before the glow of Las Vegas began to rise on the horizon, he had told her almost everything he could remember about himself—about the car and how it was stolen, about the trailer and his mother, and even, finally, about his father.

Chapter Six

———◆———

Inside Silverado Auto Body and Paint ("Special Cars for Special People") they heard the truck coming half a mile away. There was no mistaking those distinctive, quadruple air horns mounted across the roof of the cab. And no one else would lean on them like that. "The Monk," said Wayne, and Jeff and Tony laid down their tools, wiped their hands, and grinning, strolled out into the sun.

The huge purple-blue metal-flake Kenworth barreled off the highway like a smoking, howling, demented tyrannosaurus, all glinting teeth and eyes. It rolled to a panting stop outside the garage doors. Far up in the cab they could see the driver gesticulating wildly, mouthing something indistinguishable.

"Hey," Tony said, cupping his ears, "Whatdja say, Monk?" Tony was about forty, heavy-set, and there was a strain of genuine malice in his taunting.

The figure in the cab convulsed, clutched at the door, and emerged screaming. "I said get your goddamn ramp up to those back doors. Do you realize what this is costing me? Fifty-five dollars a minute, that's what it's costing me!" Monk was built like a gorilla, with the arms and chest of a weight-lifter and the hips of a fourteen-year-old. He wore a black cap—the remnants of an old fedora—that covered his ears like a cowl, and his black T-shirt hung down almost to the tops of his boots. His arms were extraordinarily hairy and were tattooed with names like Sheila, Dolores, and Jennifer. His mouth twitched spasmodically, and the furrows across his brow were not merely the normal adult worry-lines, but deep creases of chronic panic.

"Hey, Monk. Relax. C'mon in and have a coffee." Jeff was twenty-three, easily unsettled by trouble.

"Are you *crazy*? I gotta move this goddamn rig back to San Bernardino before dawn. I got a *load* to pick up. I gotta make a buck. I got *payments* to meet, man!" As he spoke, he scampered down from the cab and around to the rear, where he broke the seal, yanked down the latch, and swung the doors wide open.

Grinning, Wayne climbed the ramp. "What'd Forrie send us this time, Monk? A nice little Aspen that some dear old lady only drove to church on Sunday?" All laughed, except Monk. Wayne was the owner of Silverado and, although he was only in his mid-twenties, very much in control. When he made a joke, Jeff and Tony laughed. Then he entered the shadows of the huge trailer, and Jeff and Tony heard him whistle.

"Come on, come on! Get it out!" Monk shouted, jumping from one foot to the other and looking almost constantly at the huge watch on his left wrist. Inside, an engine kicked and started—a very powerful, supercharged engine, and a moment later a Stingray emerged into the desert sun—Dantley's Stingray with Wayne behind the wheel. Gently, respectfully, he nosed the car onto the two ramps that Jeff and Tony had laid out and let it glide down onto the gravel. He cut the engine but did not get out. "Beautiful," Jeff said softly, and the other two nodded slowly.

"Okay, okay, okay." The Monk was resealing his truck, swinging the ramp away, and pulling shipping papers from somewhere inside his clothing, all in one continuous gesture. "Lessgo, lessgo. Sign these." He pushed the papers through the Corvette's window.

"Who am I today?" Wayne asked.

"M. J. Linton," the Monk replied. "You just received a ton and a half of dried fish."

Wayne signed.

"Two-seventy," said the Monk. "Next month, Wayne, rates gotta go up. You gotta realize the kinda chances I take with the highway patrol. They nearly got me outside Barstow this trip. All it would take is one search. One! and I've had it, you know that? Finished! Kaput! Rig and all!" Behind him the big tractor breathed throatily, waiting. Diesel fumes drifted over them.

"We all got troubles, Monk." Wayne took a bill clip from the pocket of his jacket and peeled off the cash. "And here's an extra twenty because you brought such a beauty this time. Now that'll buy you five minutes, right? So come in and have a coffee."

The Monk pocketed the bills, backing up. "Thanks, Wayne, but can't do it. Gotta roll, you know. Gotta keep it rolling," and he climbed into the cab, swung the beautiful, flashing behemoth into the highway, and with a final blast of the air horns, was gone.

"Now there," said Tony, "is a man wired to the road."

Professionally, they inspected the car. They opened the hood and checked the glittering, chromeplated engine. Wayne drove it two or three miles down the highway, and when he returned Jeff asked, "So what's the verdict, do we chop it up?"

Wayne shook his head, running his hand down the Stingray's shimmering flank. "No way. Not this baby. This car is *alive*."

"So what do we do, paint it? Change the wheels? Remake it inside?"

"Nothing. I'm going to take a chance on this one," Wayne said. "I'm going to drive it just the way it is. Man"—he laughed and slapped the roof—"somebody who sure knew what he was doing rebuilt *that* machine."

Chapter Seven

———◆———

Dantley drove the last ten miles into Vegas. Vanessa had gone into the back to get changed and made up—to get, as she put it, elbowing him, "tricked up."

He was fascinated by the lights of Vegas. They were like no others he had seen. By night, most cities were just big, inverted saucers of white light, but the lights of Vegas were all colors, and they glanced off the low clouds like a shimmering surreal painting. Soon he was close enough to see the extraordinary skyline—the towering neons of the Strip, and the more subdued glowing of the big hotels, like thick, golden jewels.

"Almost there," he called back, but there was no answer, and it was not until they were actually inside the town, surrounded by the lights themselves and by the blare of loudspeaker and danceband and car sound pulsing at them through the open windows, that she emerged. Dantley was hunched over the wheel, gawking up at the hotels orbiting by, and for a moment he did not realize that she had slipped into the passenger's seat. "I'm scared," she said.

He looked. The jeans had gone, the tank top had gone, the grin and the gum had gone. Suddenly she was as garish as the lights that washed her face in their eerie, pastel colors. She had pulled on white slacks and a baby-blue sweater. Painted toenails winked through the straps of her platform shoes. Her own raven hair had vanished under a red fright-wig, her false eyelashes arched up like spiders' legs and were accentuated by strokes of mascara radiating from her eyes, and the rest of her makeup—rouge, lipstick, and powder, thick as enamel—gave her face the frozen, eerie quality of a Japanese dancer's.

Dantley stared. "Geez," he said. "Is that what you think a hooker's *supposed* to look like?"

"Yeah," she said. "Here. Las Vegas is all nostalgia."

Dantley pulled into the curb. "I gotta go, now. Good luck." He hesitated. He wanted her to laugh just once more before they parted. But she didn't. He opened the door. "Thanks for the lift. So long."

She reached across and grabbed his T-shirt so that it stretched out in a big cone. "Hey, don't go, eh, Kenny? Seriously, I really am scared." Her eyes widened. "DAMMIT, THIS IS A DEBUT, DON'T YOU REALIZE THAT?"

He climbed back in and shut the door.

"Sorry," she said. "Dammit! I didn't mean to shout at you. BUT WHAT DO I *DO*? I mean, how do I go about this? Oh, Jeez, I'm gonna be a lousy business-woman, I can see."

"You'll be okay." They were parked in the midst of casinos. From all sides came the sounds of money, and of money machines, and of the crisp, metallic voices of those who dealt in money and those who lusted after it. "I guess the thing to do is just"—he waved his hand vaguely—"drive around."

"But how much should I *ask* for?" I've never really thought about money. What do *you* think?"

"Gee, I dunno. Maybe . . ." Dantley scratched an imaginary itch between his eyes. "Maybe fifteen?"

Instantly she tensed with indignation, a lady offended. "I beg your pardon?"

"Fifty?" Dantley said.

"Yeah. That sounds about right. All right, let's go." She moved toward the waterbed.

"No! No!" Dantley groped for the door handle. He was suddenly aware of the curious gaze of passersby.

"That was a *suggestion*," he said, dropping his voice, "not an offer. I don't even *have* fifty dollars."

"Please," she pouted. "Be my first customer, Kenny. It would do wonderful things for my ego. For my professional confidence."

"No." He opened the door.

"Forty dollars."

"No."

"Thirty!"

"No."

"Twenty! For godsake, twenty!"

"No. No. Goodbye!" And he stood on the sidewalk with his knapsack hanging on one shoulder while she flung herself into the driver's seat, found first gear, and took off with a petulant squealing of tires.

Dantley watched until the van had been swallowed in the anonymous neon haze of the Strip. "So long," he said.

The commercial traveler had told him that the car was rotating on mirrors, in a hotel lobby, somewhere on the Strip, but he hadn't been able to recall which hotel. So what confronted him, Dantley had decided, was a simple process of elimination; he would go from one hotel to another until he found it. Resolutely he hefted his knapsack and began to walk.

The Strip was different than he had expected; he had not known in fact exactly *what* to expect, but in the back of his mind had been the thought that Las Vegas, for all its glitter and tinsel, would at least be a happy place, with a twenty-four-hour carnival atmosphere. What he was not prepared for was the tone of deadly *seriousness*. Everywhere he looked inside the casinos he saw serious people at the gaming tables and the machines; everyone he passed on the street had the wary, narrow-eyed expressions of hunters and hunted. He saw the hucksters, he saw the bartenders and the bargirls and the restless gamblers, he saw the chorus girls in their anonymous uniforms and the cream-faced male dancers, and he thought, my God, even their *smiles* are serious! Serious and old. Wandering the street, looking at these sad, serious, desperate old people, he formed a theory about why his car had been brought here: it was simply that it was so beautiful and so *young.* Its lines were flowing and supple and streamlined, like the contours of youth itself that these people had lost, and could buy back for only a little time, as someone at this moment was likely buying . . . And so they had captured his car and put it on a round mirror so that it would remain perfect, circling forever, and anyone who wanted to could visit that hotel and gaze at the car to their heart's content, and revel in nostalgia, which, as McGrath once told him, was just the bitter-sweet sorrow for what might have been.

But which hotel? The one he was approaching was called The Dunes; there was no mistaking it. It had a huge gold and baby-blue red-rimmed marquee that must have contained ten thousand bulbs. He went in, crossed the immense lobby, and found the desk. "Uh, excuse me."

"Yes. A room?" The desk clerk was only a little older than himself, but he wore a tuxedo, and in his eyes was the disengaged calm of an old, old man.

"I'm looking for a car," Dantley said.

Smoothly, the clerk withdrew the proffered card. "Garage is one floor down," he said. "Elevators on your right, car rentals . . ."

"No, no. This car is a little special. It's in a hotel lobby. On a mirror."

A man wearing thick rings and with pouches under his eyes stepped past Dantley and reached across the desk, palm up. The clerk gave him a key.

"A Stingray," Dantley said. "'Seventy-three."

"Not here, sir," said the clerk, smiling as blandly as if Dantley had not been a sweaty, stringy-haired kid with red eyes and a grungy Marine knapsack slung over one shoulder. "Try the others."

61

The Sahara was next. In its lobby there was a miniature oasis with a comatose camel hunkering beside it. Two Arab guests regarded the display skeptically. On his way to the desk, Dantley was stopped by a small, trimly dressed man whose nervous hands moved incessantly. "Excuse me," the man whispered, "but you look like a winner." He guided Dantley to a corner where a woman in a low-cut gown was waiting. The woman smiled and turned toward him; her bosom swelled, straining against the top of the gown and engulfing Dantley's gaze. "Let me show you something," the little man whispered, detaching his cufflinks.

"Why are you whispering?" Dantley whispered, still staring at the bosom, which had now begun to undulate with a marvelous, pneumatic life of its own.

"Shh," the little man whispered. "Private. See these?"

"What?"

"These. Hey, *these!* Solid gold! Problem is, I need cash in a hurry. So, they're yours for seventy dollars.

Absentmindedly, still staring, Dantley shook his head. Ordinarily he would simply have walked away; but he was caught, riveted. Glancing around, the man tugged a watch from his wrist. "Everything for a hundred," he whispered. "What d'yuh say? You gonna say no to a *Pul*sar?"

"No," Dantley said, still staring. "I mean yes. I mean, I don't want anything—cufflinks, watch, anything."

"Nothing?" The woman raised an eyebrow.

"Okay, no hard feelings." The man had taken the girl's arm and was leading her away. "Come on, Jennifer. It's clear the gentleman doesn't want anything this evening, didn't you hear him?" He replaced his watch and cufflinks and hurried the girl out through the revolving door. On the street he rifled Dantley's wallet in a twinkling, slipped the bills up his sleeve, and tossed the leather husk into the trash can. "Kid won't miss it for hours," he said to the girl, and they both laughed softly.

At the Sands, Dantley found an intimidating clerk behind the desk. He *knew* that this guy would speak with a British accent, something that had always terrified him, and so he moved toward the first young bellhop he saw. The kid had pimples and a permanent, cynical, curled-lip expression. "Where the hell have you been?" he asked.

"Huh?"

"Come on. Come on," the bellhop said. "Jeff told me you'd be here at eight and it's ten after. Mr. 408's up there waitin! Hell, he's phoned down *twice* in the past ten minutes."

"Wait a minute. I'm just looking for a car."

"*Forget* the car, for crissake! We'll look after that later. Just get up there! And listen! He held up fingers. Number one: I get cash, not chips. Number two: Don't try to duck me on the way out, okay, because I got guys who'll break your fingers. . . Hey . . . Hey!"

Dantley had been backing away from this person, and now he turned and ran back through the vast lobby, out the door, and into the street.

He was still walking fast and glancing over his shoulder when he found himself outside the Silver Bird. This time he approached more warily, determined not to enter if he could avoid it. He was aware of the doorman watching him approach. Only the doorman's eyes moved—sideways and down—and fixed themselves on Dantley. The doorman was enormously fat, and the upthrust of his double chins gave him a kind of permanent grin and squint. He stood with his arms behind his back, and he rocked gently on his toes, back and forth. He was a full-blooded Indian.

"Excuse me." The top of Dantley's head came to the man's armpit. The doorman was gazing out now, far far out over the roofs of passing cars, over the Strip, over the desert, to the hills beyond. Dantley felt like a very small child again; he almost tugged at the hem of

63

the man's jacket. "Excuse me. I know this sounds a bit silly, but do you have a car inside?"

The man nodded; the folds of skin under his jaw rolled and rippled like water rolling off a whale's back.

"I mean, a full-size automobile. On a mirror."

Again the man nodded. "Insi-i-i-de . . ." His voice was high and trailed off like the cry of a distant hawk. "On your left. Before the lounge-e-e."

Small, cold fingers ran very quickly up and down Dantley's spine. It was here! His car! All his exhaustion, all the emotional heights and pits that he had experienced in the past twenty-four hours, all the fear that he had lived with, encountering one crazy after another—all dropped away from him. He felt very calm, even heroic. He didn't know what he was going to do when he stepped through the glass doors. He had no idea how he was going to prove that the car was his, that it had been stolen, and he had not even thought about how he would extricate it from the lobby of the Silver Bird Hotel, and get it out of Las Vegas and wound out on Highway 15, heading home. All he knew for certain was that he would do it. And when he got to Los Angeles he would get it washed, he would tune it until it purred, and he would drive it very slowly into the trailer park and up to the door of his mother's place, and he would tap a knuckle on the door and say, "Hey, in there. How'dja like to take a little ride . . ."

"Don't hold up the traffic, son." The doorman's squeaky voice needled him back to reality; there was a middle-aged couple, all rhinestone, fucshia, and Hawaiian prints, scowling behind him. He pushed the door. He went in. He saw in the distance, across the vast lobby, a low red shape with orange flames licking back up its fuselage, turning slowly under caressing spotlights that flickered up from the mirror and splashed in ten thousand glinting pieces across the ceiling. A sparse crowd surrounded it. The tips of his fingers went numb, and the numbness spread over his palms and wrists as it had when Danny Kupensky had pitched a beanball at him when they were nine years old. He moved toward the car like a man in deep water. The subdued sounds of the lobby washed around him. His knapsack fell away. A blissful grin spread across his face. His arms reached out to touch, to embrace . . .

But something was wrong. In fact, everything was wrong except the colors. The turntable revealed a short, arched profile, with a chopped-off tail. And in front, a tiny, flat-black grille! "A 280-Z," Dantley said, afraid for an instant that he was going to cry. "A *Datsun!*" And, indeed, that's what it was, a 1977 tricked up to look like an illustration in *Car Craft*.

Underneath was a sign: "Silverado Auto Body and Paint—Special Cars for Special People."

Dantley was numb all over, but it was not the numbness of excitement now, but of fatigue. He was exhausted. He could taste bitterness like rust, like copper. It took a huge effort to push through the glass doors. The dry heat of the desert night gripped him. "Forgot something, son," said a squeaky voice, and he turned around to see a bellhop dropping his knapsack beside the doorman's feet as if it were covered with ants. He picked it up and slung it over his shoulder. "Thanks," he said, but the bellhop had gone back inside. The Indian doorman did not look at him; he was gazing far out over the neons and the desert to the distant hills, and he was rocking, toes and heels, toes and heels. "Keep lookin', son," he said. "Keep lookin'."

Suddenly, Dantley was ravenously hungry. He had never known such hunger, and he realized, beginning to dog-trot toward a neon EATS sign half a block away, that he had not eaten since he had a sandwich in the trailer before leaving Los Angeles, twenty-six hours earlier. The delectable odors of cheap, greasy, starchy food reached out and drew him toward the counter. He sagged onto a stool. "Three chili dogs, two orders of fries, and a double-chocolate malted."

He hunched up, waiting. He tried not to think of

65

anything; he wanted most of all to keep back the disappointment that lay, huge and waiting, just beyond the edges of his mind.

The only other customer was a tiny man with thick glasses who sat at the far end of the counter, eating a huge steak, grinning idiotically, occasionally giggling. Dantley glanced at him warily; what he did not need right now was to be accosted by another freak. No, he did not need that. "Hi," said the man, waving. "How ya doin?" His glasses were so thick that his eyes seemed to be moving in large neon pools of glycerine. Dantley raised a finger.

"Four-eighty," said the counterman, plunking down plates of gorgeous, hot food in front of him.

And it was then, reaching into his hip pocket, that Dantley discovered that his wallet had been stolen. A sensation like a small electrical shock ran through him, up the center, but nothing else. He was too hungry, too tired. "You're not going to believe this," he said to the counterman, but the man had already begun to gather up the plates.

"I'll believe it," he used. "You tell me, I'll believe it."

"My wallet's gone."

"I believe it," said the counterman.

The customer at the far end of the counter, smiling and eating, watched with interest.

Dantley laid both hands, palms up and pleading, on the counter. "Look, man, I gotta have some food. Please. Let me wash dishes for it."

"No dishes anymore, kid. All plastic. Beat it."

"Aw," said the little man with glasses, "why don't you give the kid his food, for goshsakes. Can't you see he's famished?"

The counterman turned a baleful gaze on him. "Famished got nothin' to do with it. Money got everything to do with it."

"Money!" The little man looked incredulous. "But

66

you're surrounded by money! All you have to do is hold out your hand."

"Yeah? Well I been holdin' out my hand in this goddamn town for five years, and look what it's got me: a goddamn apron!"

The customer polished off the remnants of his steak and drew out his wallet. He was still smiling; the wallet was very fat. "You a gambling man?"

"How d'ya think I won this apron? This place? I put a perfectly good Bronco up against it."

"Okay, let's make it interesting." He laid a twenty-dollar bill on the table. "Either I'll pay you for the kid's supper or I'll give you four-to-one odds on a toss. Which is it?"

The counterman shrugged. Into his eye had come the calculating, unhappy, greedy gleam that Dantley had seen everywhere since his arrival. "Why not," said the man. He extracted a coin from the till and flipped it.

"Heads," said the customer.

The coin landed on the counter, spun, and flopped over, revealing the impressive profile of Thomas Jefferson. "Shit!"

The customer chuckled and tucked his bill back into the wallet which he had kept out. His eyes rolled happily in the multicolored glycerine. "I love it! Eat up, kid!" The counterman plunked the dishes down again, looking as if he smelled rotten fish.

"What's the catch?" Dantley asked.

"No catch. Honest. When I finish this coffee I'm leaving this town for good, and I just wanted to prove it one last time before I went—I can't lose!"

Later, when he had finished eating, as Dantley walked his benefactor to his car, the man said, "Really, it's the goddamnest thing. I've been here for eighteen hours—just dropped in on the way home, you know—and I've won eighteen thousand dollars! Incredible! I've heard about things like that happening, but I never thought it would happen to me. Almost makes you believe in God, eh?"

"You're not going to L.A. by any chance?"

"Nope. Just gonna run this baby back to Avis and then I'll grab the first plane back to Portland, one happy pharmacist, I can tell you! Let me give you some advice, kid: quit while you're ahead."

"Thanks," Dantley said. "I'll try to remember. Thanks for the meal."

The man got into his car and started the engine. He looked up at Dantley, his eyes huge pools. "You're in a bad way, aren't you. Tell you what, I'll pass my winning streak on to you. Here."

"A two-dollar bill?"

"That's what I *started* with. I told myself I'd only spend fifty of those, no more, no less, but I never got past the first one. So long, kid." He put the car into gear and was gone; half a block away, Dantley could hear him whooping and laughing through the open windows.

He began to walk. He had exactly two dollars and a quarter in his pocket—the bill his benefactor had just given him and the coin Kootz had handed to him at parting. Walking backward, he looked wistfully at the hotels—the hotels with the soft glow of lamps behind their drapes, and their soft beds, and their soft, warm water . . . He could, at that moment, imagine nothing better than to be wafted on a silent elevator up, up, and to go down the silent broadloom of the halls, and into his room, and to sleep. Sleep.

He kept walking. The lights grew fewer, the buildings sparser and lower, hunkering down on nondescript concrete-block foundations. Close behind them, under a scraggle of weeds, fences, discarded plastic toys, and old tires, the desert began. After half an hour he came to a gas station with a few U-Haul trailers parked behind. There was no one around. Occasionally, cars passed at great speed. He drifted in, skirting the side of the building, and checked out the trailers one by one.

The fifth or sixth was unlocked and—magnificently!—it contained a small stack of furniture pads. He climbed in, shut the doors behind him, and wrapped himself up. It was cold, now. He shivered for awhile before the food and the furniture pad began to warm him and then he drifted into that stage of euphoric images that precedes sleep.

Foremost amid those images was Vanessa—not the Vanessa of the fright-wig and the lacquered makeup, but the earlier one, the one who worked on the barter system, laughing, talking, and—miraculously—*listening*, her black hair brushing her freckled shoulder as she turned toward him. He was delighted to see her. "Hi," he said. She waved, a finger movement on her right hand, and then, looking at him all the time, smiling, she began to undress. Behind her, one by one, the freaks, weirdos, crazies, and assorted monsters who had crowded Kenny Dantley's day took their bows and departed. Vanessa remained; but before she had finished her performance, he had fallen asleep, and if anyone had invaded the privacy of his trailer and the comforting warmth of his furniture pad, they would have seen that he was smiling.

Dawn came to Las Vegas. Tired gamblers, winners and losers, emerged from the casinos to find their celebrations and their consolations. Outside the Sahara Hotel, a small man in a blue uniform began methodically to sweep up the butts, packages, plastic cups, and other detritus that had been scattered during the night. Ordinary people awoke, and had coffee in ordinary kitchens, and found their way to ordinary jobs. The neons went off. Because it was Sunday, somewhere in the distance church bells rang—or rather, recordings of bells rang through amplifiers on church roofs. Probably it was one of these recordings that awakened Kenny Dantley.

There were flies in the trailer; several had already strolled across his face. He pulled himself out of the furniture pad, and after a minute or so, managed to

69

collect himself and his knapsack and emerge from the trailer into the glaring sun of a Nevada morning. The owner of the station was just arriving, and he watched indignantly as Dantley shut the doors of the trailer, crossed the lot, and headed out toward the highway. "Morning," Dantley called, but the man did not reply.

Despite his appearance, a car stopped for him, a Toronado with all the windows up. *Air conditioning*, he thought. *All the way to L.A.!* He slung his knapsack and began to run, and he had actually begun to open the door of the Toronado when he saw it.

His car.

Unmistakably his car.

Unmistakably.

It passed too fast for him to see the driver, but the car, the CAR was his, glorious in the morning sun, moving with controlled elegance toward the center of town.

Without a word of thanks to the driver who had stopped for him, he slammed the door of the Toronado, dropped the knapsack, and began to run.

Chapter Eight

———◆———

He couldn't see the driver. The car was moving at a steady twenty-five or thirty miles per hour, but there were lights ahead and with luck they might stay red long enough for him to catch up. He had never been an athlete; within half a block he was winded, but adrenalin had begun to course through him, and when he saw the light ahead turn red, trapping the car, he redoubled his efforts. There was no grace in Dantley's running, very little coordination, and only minimal control. He ran like a spastic ostrich, feet slapping, head rolling, arms lashing out at crazy angles. Pedestrians shrank into doorways at his approach.

He was only a hundred yards behind when the light changed and the car moved ahead. For a few more wild paces he tried to keep up but couldn't. He caromed off a wall, staggered into a lamp post, reeled backward, bent over, gulping for air and trying unsuccessfully to curse. He seemed like a man in the throes of a serious fit. "Stuh . . . Stuh . . . gadan . . . theeth . . . !"

At one point he took a desperate shortcut, sprinting behind a board fence into what he thought was an empty corner lot, only to find himself surrounded by broken and discarded neons. Too late to retreat, he danced precariously along the flank of a long, slim sign. At the end, a grinning cowboy fifteen feet tall loomed upon him, forcing a quick right turn. A tattered chorus line kicked him back to the left, and a monstrous roulette wheel, in which he lost his balance and went sprawling, spun him around on its creaky machinery. He climbed out dazed and dizzy, reeling off in what he thought was the right direction, only to be stopped by a sign that said ENTRANCE, and then by one that said ALICE GALLERY, and then by a vacuous, ten-foot face of Colonel Sanders. He no longer knew in which direction he was going, or where the Stingray was, and when he finally extricated himself, squeezing through a narrow alley between an arching sign that said CASINO and one that said MINT, he emerged on the road again. For a few mindless paces he ran in the wrong direction, and whirled around just in time to see the Corvette vanishing around a corner three blocks away.

He staggered off in pursuit, pains piercing his chest with every gasp, despair like lead in his stomach. By the time he reached the corner he discovered that he had, incredibly, narrowed the gap—whoever was driving the car was obviously in no hurry. And then, miraculously, at the next block a light changed red and the Stingray stopped, right flasher working. Guessing desperately, he plunged down an alley on his right, and was rewarded, when he was halfway through, by seeing the car glide past the end, much closer. The sound of its exhaust throbbed briefly, enticingly, between the narrow walls. Dantley shot out the end of the alley like a human projectile, swung right, and saw that the car, just ahead, was slowly approaching a set of several railroad tracks on which switch engines shunted back and forth, working their way through the various loading stages of an industrial complex. Very slowly the car began to move across the tracks, got to the middle, and stalled. Dantley was close enough to hear, through the roaring of his own breathing and the pounding of blood through his ears, the fruitless whirring of the starter motor. "Don't start!" he begged, but in the next second he heard two sounds which chilled him despite the sweat that was washing off him: the unmistakable BWAMP BWAMP of a big diesel locomotive, and the musical dingdong as the warning lights sprang into life. "Start!" he screamed. "For godsakes start!" He was talking to the car, not the driver. He was addressing it as a sentient being, his creation, which was about to be mashed into a sickening tangle of glass, steel, and fiberglass.

The starter motor ticked over desperately.

BWAAAAMP!

Staggering forward, Dantley frantically pushed air at the car. "Go! Go! Don't flood it, you idiot!"

BWAMP! BWAMP! BWAAAMP!

And the engine caught. In the last possible seconds the car lurched forward and down the embankment off the tracks, and Dantley collapsed onto his hands and knees, sobbing with relief and exhaustion. Two diesels and 108 hopper cars of manganese lumbered inexorably past, and by the time the caboose came to Kenny Dantley he had managed to get back on his feet and to return the trainman's noncommittal wave. The wig-wag stopped. A decrepit fruit-and-vegetable truck labored up the incline and shuddered across the tracks. There was no sign of the Corvette.

"Right-hand drive, you say," said the desk sergeant, looking up from Dantley's newsprint photograph. "Shouldn't be hard to find a right-hand drive Corvette those colors." He began to fill in a form. "License number?"

"I didn't get it," Dantley said. "I wasn't close enough. But that car is here. MY car! Listen, all you gotta do is block the highways and then work in toward the center of town." He moved his hands together until the fingers locked. "Dragnet. You got him!"

"Your full name."

"But look," Dantley said, "you gotta do it *now*. Really. Tomorrow will be too late. Use the radio."

The sergeant looked up with the profound weariness of a man who has heard it all before, and seen it, many times. "Leave it to us, son. We're a very efficient police department. Your name?"

Las Vegas
July 23

Dear Mr. McGrath:

I figgered that Id just let you know that Im here and that the cars here too and I know because I seen it, and Im gonna stay here and keep lookin until I find it and bring it back. So you can tell the school board not to worry, okay? and the insurance company. The police here know because I reported it but Im not even sure they believed me because Im a kid and who pays any attenshun to kids espeshuly ones that look like me. But it doesn't matter anyhow because I'll do it myself. You'll see in a few days Ill come drivin back there in that Vette and Ill give it back to you and when I do theres just one favor I want to ask, so be ready for me to ask you a favor. Okay?

Mr. Redman always said when you change a topic change a paragraph, and thats one of the things I remember because he said it was like changing gears. So I guess Im changin the topic because I just wanna tell you that this is a very good place to stay away from, unless you've gotta come on business, because its full of freaks, loonies, psychos, and all kinds of bad people. The cars are great but the people are nuts. Maybe its the desert that does funny things to them, or maybe its the money and the gambling, but they sure are crazies, they sure are. Dont worry about me though because I can look after myself. So please don't worry.

Your friend,
K. Dantley

When he had finished writing this letter, Dantley switched off his flashlight and worked his way down between the folds of the furniture cover, preparing to go to sleep. He felt pretty good; he felt as if luck was on his side. That afternoon, almost flat broke except for the two-dollar bill that the happy pharmacist had given him, he had been surprised by the discovery of a quarter in his left pocket (the lucky side, he always called it) and for a moment he could not recall how it got there; then he remembered Kootz flipping it to him—play the slots for me. He had done that, and he had won some money. Not a great deal, but $3.75, enough to buy supper, two batteries for the flashlight, a big stamped postcard, and a Bic pen. At dusk, when he felt he could not search one more lot, he returned to the trailer and set up house. He felt right at home; all that was missing was his mother crying out in her sleep. He didn't know why he had written to McGrath instead of his mother; he didn't even think about it. It just seemed natural—to write to McGrath about the car. He knew he would find it; he knew that it was just a question of time until their paths crossed again.

He settled more or less comfortably into the furniture pad. It warmed him. He began to fall asleep, and again there came to him the enticing images of Vanessa—Vanessa laughing, Vanessa walking with her long strides, Vanessa undressing . . .

At first he controlled these images, summoned them and used them as he wished; but with increasing drowsiness he began to lose this control, and more and more the images gained a life of their own, so that Vanessa was no longer performing as he wished her to perform. He became a mere spectator in an unpredictable display—a display which very soon involved other people. To his astonishment, his mother was there, and his father, and they were sweeping past in the Corvette convertible, laughing, and their clothes were as brilliantly white as the car. Yet, despite the speed, they did not pass him; rather, it was the blurred world which streamed by in the background while they themselves stayed still forever, laughing, waving to him, beckoning him to join them; but no matter how desperately he ran after them, they and the car remained elusively beyond his reach.

They faded; Vanessa returned. And this time she was not a performer but a lover, and at the touch of her lips his frustration and sadness merged into passionate desire . . .

He awoke abruptly, realizing two things in quick succession: first, that he had been asleep, and second that he had had . . .

HE HAD HAD A DREAM!
HE HAD DREAMED!

He sat bolt upright. So *that* was what it was like! That was what happened when people dreamed—some deep part of them came awake and entertained them with personal movies! Extraordinary! He felt as if he had just joined the human race. He began to laugh; he felt . . .

Outside, a door slammed. He remembered then what it was that had wakened him; it was the sound of a vehicle pulling in close to his U-Haul trailer. It must be the police, or the owner of the station; he tensed and lay silent, waiting to be hassled. But no one bothered him; instead, the locked door of the ladies' rest room was rattled, then kicked. "Shit! Goddam!"

Dantley sat up. It was Vanessa. He was sure. He stayed still, listening, but there were no further words, only a sob, then another, then a soft, muffled weeping. Wearing his furniture pad like an oversize shawl, he opened the door of the trailer and dropped down. His sneakers made sucking sounds on the asphalt. It *was* her; she was sitting on the concrete step and she was crying. At the whispering sound of Dantley's dragging furniture pad she looked up and, when she saw who it was, managed a wan smile. "Hi," she said. She had been beaten up. Both eyes were black and swollen, there were ugly bruises on her neck and jaw, and her sweater was ripped. The fright-wig had vanished; her own hair was disheveled and gray with dirt.

"Hi," Dantley said. He shuffled a little closer. "What happened?"

"You wouldn't want to hear about it. Really. It's too sordid. Really sick! And now," she said, spreading her arms dramatically, "now I can't even get into a can to wash up."

Dantley looked at the two doors, frowning slightly. They bore black silhouettes, one a panted figure, one skirted. "Why don't you use the men's? I know it's open. I been using it."

She hesitated. "That'd be all I'd need—some ape to come in there and beat me up again. No thanks."

"Nobody's gonna come in here tonight. It's closed. There're no lights. Besides"—he pulled the furniture cover more tightly around him—"I'll stand guard."

"What'll you say if somebody does come?"

"I'll warn them. I'll say that my friend's in there sick—really, really sick with something catching. I'll kinda arch my neck like this, and ask him if he knows the symptoms of meningitis."

She almost smiled. She brushed the tears away with the back of her hand, swung her hair away from her shoulders, and went into the men's room. The light and the exhaust fan went on simultaneously, and a few moments later Dantley heard water running into the basin. He pulled the furniture pad more tightly around him and sat down on the concrete step. He shivered. Occasionally cars swished past in the deserted street, but none turned in. From several blocks away came the metallic sounds of the Strip. But here it was quiet, almost serene. For a little time, at least, they were out of it.

"Hey," she called out," I need a towel. Will you get it? Inside. Bottom drawer of the bureau."

He entered the van, found the towel, and hung it, valet-style, over the bare arm that appeared through a crack in the door. The fingers on the end of the arm

77

waved thanks, and the door closed again. "Find your car?"

"Yeah. Yeah, I found it." He was seized with a sudden urge to talk, to tell her everything. "But it was an accident, you know? I mean, it wasn't where I thought it was going to be, and I nearly missed it."

"So, if you've got your Stingray, why are you sleeping in a U-Haul trailer?"

"Well, I found it, sort of, but I haven't really *got* it, know what I mean?"

"No."

"Well, like . . ." Dantley shuffled from foot to foot, clinging to his furniture blanket and frowning at the door. "Really, I just *saw* it, going by, and I know it's somewhere in Vegas."

"So you're gonna stay until you've found it again, right? Until you get it."

"Right." He hesitated a moment, listening to some final sounds of washing from inside. "How . . . how about you? Are you gonna leave now?"

"Leave!" The door burst open and Vanessa emerged, still toweling around her ears. "Hell, no! I've just begun. All professional people have trouble at first, especially women. Didn't you know that? And just because I get slapped around by some kink doesn't mean that I'm gonna *give up*, for godsake!" She was walking toward the van as she talked, nylon bathrobe whispering around her legs. At the step she paused. "Listen, Danny . . ."

"Kenny."

"Kenny. Why don't you come in and spend the night? God, it beats a U-Haul, doesn't it? And besides, I could use a little comforting, know what I mean? It's been quite a day."

"Well . . ."

"Oh, come *on*. You *know* you want to. So don't be a hypocrite."

"Well, okay. Maybe just for awhile." He followed her in.

"Sure." Smiling, she closed the door behind him. Inside it was warm and soft. There was milk in the refrigerator and soft music on the tape deck. Vanessa continued to smile at him while she dried her hair, but when she sat beside him on the waterbed he edged away and sat on the shag carpet beside the fridge, his back to the wall and his furniture pad wrapped around him like armor. His heart was racing. He was immobilized—drawn to her by the erotic aftermath of his first dream and, as he had been all his life, terrified by the mystery of women and by their dreadful capacity to hurt.

"Hey," she said, looking at him incredulously, "you *afraid* of me?"

"Naw. Naw. Just a little more comfortable over here, that's all." He was watching her like a cornered animal.

"Hey! Wait a minute, wait a minute!" She forgot about her hair and leaned toward him. "This is an honor."

"Why? Whadya mean?"

"You've never . . . Not even . . . Hey, really, I'm gonna be your first woman, right? That's true, isn't it?"

"Naw, naw." Dantley waved his hands palms out as if wiping off a blackboard, but his heels were digging deeper into the shag rug, pushing him back hard against the wall, away from Vanessa. "Naw, I've been through this lots of times; lots and lots of times."

She smiled. "Well then," she said, and began to loosen her bathrobe. Dantley twitched as if he had been stabbed by a large pin.

"Thing is!" he shouted, then cleared his throat and tried again more quietly. "Thing is, I'm really tired right now, you know? Really, really stroked out. So good night, okay? Good night." And he lay down and rolled over abruptly, face to the wall, furniture pad clutched tightly around him like a protective shell.

Dumbfounded, Vanessa stared at his back, still holding the cord of her bathrobe. Then, very deliberately and thoughtfully, she undressed and went to bed. For several minutes she stared at the ceiling—shrugged. "Vanessa." she said, "you got a long way to go."

On the floor, long after she had gone to sleep, Dantley lay staring at the carpeted wall of the van, listening to the gentle rhythm of her breathing. "Hey," Dantley whispered. "I had a dream. I dreamed about you." But there was no reply.

By morning, prodded by offended pride, Vanessa had made certain business decisions which she announced to Dantley when he awoke.

"I'm a working girl, right?"

"Right."

"A professional."

"Well, I dunno . . ." Dantley was folding up the furniture pad, preparing to leave.

"Okay, take my word for it. A professional. So what that means is that I gotta charge a fee, right? I mean, friendship is friendship but business is business. Right?"

"Right. So?"

"So twenty bucks."

"*Me?*"

"You."

"But I didn't *do* anything."

"You stayed the whole night; it should be forty."

"But I haven't *got* twenty. Besides, you invited me."

"Of course I invited you, dummy! It's my business to invite men." Dantley considered. He could see her point, but something deep inside him had been hurt, betrayed. For a little while he had thought that he had found a friend. For a little while he had thought that he might, if Vanessa were patient, be able to overcome his paralyzing embarrassment, and then . . . For a little while—all night, in fact—he had forgotten about the Corvette. "Look," he said, "I just haven't got twenty bucks. All I've got is two. I'll give that to you. It's lucky. So here. Good luck, Vanessa."

She shrugged and took it. "Okay. Thanks. And good luck to you, too. Listen, if I see the car . . ."

"Yeah. Let me know. So long."

She raised two fingers—peace—and then, with an excessive revving of the engine, she was gone. Dantley watched the van out of sight, his face very hard. He shivered and picked up the furniture pad.

"That your last two bucks?"

"Huh?" Dantley spun around to discover a heavy-set, middle-aged man in blue trousers and blue shirt with an oval Exxon patch on the pocket. It was the filling-station owner he had seen the previous morning at a distance. He was leaning against a corner of the building, and his eyes were shaded by a blue peaked cap, again with the Exxon insignia. "Interesting," the man said. "Interesting way to start the morning. Never know what you're gonna find. Frankly, I'd say you got a deal, but my question was, was that your last two bucks? Because if it was, you're gonna need a job, right? And I need a gopher and gas jockey. Last guy quit yesterday. Whatdya say?"

Dantley shrugged. He glanced out at the road, a main entrance to Vegas, along which many cars were already moving, gleaming and flashing in the low, morning sun. He touched the emptiness of his trouser pocket. "Okay," he said. "Sure. Why not?"

"Name's Gil," said the man, offering his hand.

"Kenny," said Dantley, taking it. He already liked this man; he had noted a distinct resemblance to Mr. McGrath.

Chapter Nine

The next week was the most disillusioning that Kenny had ever experienced.

He had accepted Gil's job offer because he needed money, and because the station was in a good location to watch for the Stingray, and also because he had liked the man, and trusted him. He had thought that he would run an honest garage. On the very first day, however, he learned how wrong he had been. After the first flurry of early-morning business had subsided, Gil motioned him into the shop where a row of old batteries sat on newspaper. He indicated a spraygun. "Know how to use one of those, don'cha, Kenny?"

"Sure."

"Good boy. Now then, here's what goes in it," and winking, he handed Kenny a quart can.

He shook it. "Not paint."

"Stove black. Now, what you're gonna do in the next half-hour is make some nice new batteries for me. Understand, Kenny? Get the picture?"

"Yeah, I understand. Sure." Listlessly he tossed the can, caught it, tossed it again. He nudged a battery with his toe.

"Any problems?" Gil was watching him closely.

"No, I guess not."

"Well, it's up to you. You can either spray those batteries or take a walk down the road. But if you decide to go, just remember that there's no town in this country where the competition's tougher, and you're not gonna find any lily-white station operators around

Scenes on the following pages are from the MGM production, CORVETTE SUMMER, released by United Artists.

Mark Hamill as Kenny Dantley and Annie Potts as Vanessa.

Dantley and his auto shop class, with teacher McGrath (Eugene Roche), save a battered Corvette from the wrecking crusher.

Dantley's dream car takes shape in a clay model.

After months of hard work—roll-out!

Top-hatted Kootz (Danny Bonaduce) shows off aboard the Corvette along Van Nuys Boulevard.

Mr. McGrath and Dantley are worried: where's the Corvette?

Dantley hitches a ride to Las Vegas
with Vanessa (Annie Potts).

Dantley finds Vanessa working in a Vegas drive-in.

Dantley commandeers a bicycle to chase his stolen sports car through the streets of Las Vegas.

Vanessa shows Kenny how she feels.

Vanessa has turned into the chic Rosalind. There's a new man in her life.

Kenny fights for his life.

Kenny rescues Vanessa from a life of sin.

Dantley and Vanessa think they may be in love.

here, believe me. Dog eat dog, that's the name of the game, m'boy, and I'm winnin' at it. Now you gonna help me cut a few corners or not?"

"Sure. No problem." Kenny said, and he began to fill the spraygun.

"Cutting corners" meant a number of things to Gil, as Kenny was to learn. It meant spraying batteries black and mufflers silver—("Beautiful. Beautiful! You keep up this kinda work, Kenny, and I'll promote you to salesman in no time.") It meant dropping Alka-Seltzer tablets into the batteries of unsuspecting owners when he checked under the hood. ("Part of a salesman's job. You're a salesman now—batteries, tires . . .") It meant wearing a ring that was scalpel-sharp on the bottom. (". . . fan belts and radiator hoses.") It meant, in fact, destroying as many car parts as possible in order to replace them with Gil's "new" products; and, ideally, it meant getting cars inside, up on the hoist. ("By God, Kenny, once you get 'em in there there's no end to what you can do to 'em!") It meant, in short, destroying; Kenny had never liked destruction; he had already discovered that he preferred building—in his opinion, there was altogether too much destruction in the world, and altogether too much hurt, and that it might be better for man to build.

Nevertheless, under Gil's watchful eye—because, after all, he did need the money and because from Gil's station he had a good, clear view of a stretch of main highway—he did use the ring, and the tablets, and other useful tools of destruction as often as he felt it was absolutely necessary to do so. They remained a last resort, to be used only when there were no legitimate repairs, and he reserved them even then for customers he definitely did not like—narrow-eyed men with high collars who called him "kid," men accompanied by weeping children, and fat, careless men who had clearly abused the fine pieces of machinery their automobiles had once been. He reserved Gil's tricks for such people, trying as much as possible to spare those customers who he had decided were innocent, or, at least, more innocent.

That was why, after he had been at the station for a full week, he hesitated when Gil told him to slit the fan belt of an old Dodge driven by a disheveled and obviously harassed woman with three small children. "It's not fair, Gil. It just isn't."

"Fair! Fair! Who said anything about fair? I just told you to do a little job on her fan belt. Damn it, kid, it's a slow day!"

"Let her go. I'll make it up to you later. Damn husband's probably run away and left her, kids aren't getting anything to eat . . ."

"Problems, problems. Everybody's got problems. Who hasn't? But in this world, kid, you gotta learn: it's dog eat dog and everybody out for himself. Remember that."

Dantley was examining the woman's credit card. Outside, a hood slammed down. "Hey, Gil."

"Don't argue, just *do* it!"

"But . . ."

"No buts! Listen, do you want a job or don't you?"

"But she doesn't have enough money even to pay for her gas and oil. Look at this. Credit card's out of date."

"Wha . . ."

A door slammed. The car roared into life and raced away from the pumps, tires smoking. Gil ran out of the office, shaking his fist and shouting, but he was far too late; already the Dodge had reached the highway and was quickly engulfed in traffic. Gil cursed, stamped his foot, slapped his knee.

Dantley dropped the credit card into the trash can. "We could send her a bill," he said.

"You"—Gil spun around, pointing—"you are a smart-ass, you know that?"

"Every man for himself, Gil. Take or get taken, remember?"

"Yeah? Well, we're just gonna see how much got

taken, m'boy, and then we'll talk a little more. But I'll tell you one thing, it ain't gonna come out of *my* pocket, just remember that." He snatched a piece of paper and a blunt pencil off his desk and returned outside to make his list. "Look after that customer." he said over his shoulder. But Dantley was not listening. He was not, in fact, paying any attention at all; he was gazing over Gil's head to the highway, where a gorgeous cherry-red and white van was slowing, its right-turn signal working, preparing to glide down the ramp and into the station. Vanessa!

"The customer!" Gil shouted, pointing to the pumps where the driver of a rusty Mustang was beginning to tap his horn impatiently.

"Yeah," Dantley said. "Yeah." And he began to move toward the van, stopping to untie and tie a shoe-lace when he realized that he was in danger of letting his eagerness show.

"I found it," Vanessa said, leaning out before the van had come to a full stop.

Dantley stopped in his tracks. "God? You found God?"

"No, dummy." She hit the door with her fist. "Your car!"

"My . . . How do you know?"

She sighed heavily and glanced heavenward. "Stingray, right? Orange and red? Superior Dynamo mags? Right-hand drive?"

"Right! Yes!"

"I saw it. Hop in."

"Ten gallons!" Gil was shouting, waving his slip of paper, striding toward them across the blacktop. "That's what she took me for. And four quarts of Pennzoil, one quart of Quaker State, and two sets of wipers. And I just want to let you know, Kenny m'boy that all of that is going to come out of your next week's paycheck."

"Okay." Grinning, Dantley rounded the rear of the van, winking at Gil as he passed. Exasperated, the customer in the Mustang started his engine and peeled out.

"And that!" Gil exploded. "That too! Ten gallons at least!"

"Okay, Gil." Dantley swung up into the passenger's seat. "As a matter of fact, why don't you just keep all next week's paycheck and put it where the light won't shine on it!" Honking cars had begun to cluster around the pumps.

"Wha . . . Listen, you get your ass down here and . . ."

"And this week's too," Dantley said. "I quit. Oh. Here. This belongs to you." He leaned across Vanessa to drop the knife-ring into Gil's hand. "Hit it," he said to Vanessa, leaning back into the deep comfort of the seat. She did that, sweeping past Gil's expostulations with her nose in the air.

For several minutes neither spoke. Vanessa drove, Dantley rode with his head back and his eyes closed. Then he said, "You know, it would be good to find one person in this town—just one—who wasn't a crook."

"You'd be lucky," she said. "Anywhere."

"Yeah." He nodded, frowning, thinking of Mr. McGrath. "Yeah." Then he sat up abruptly, remembering what it was that had brought Vanessa back to him. "Where's the car?"

"Main parking lot," she said. "Flamingo Hotel."

"Okay," Dantley shouted, pounding the door. "Let's go! Let's go!" For a moment he paused, staring at Vanessa, actually looking at her for the first time since they had left the service station. She was dressed in white slacks, white tunic. Her hair had subtly and enticingly changed its color. She was carefully made up and manicured, and compared to the battered and bedraggled creature he had last seen emerging from the men's room at the station, she was splendid—but splendid in a cool, sexless way he could not understand.

"What're you supposed to be, a nurse?"

86

"Beautician," she said, shifting adroitly. She winked at him. "Got a cover job. How do I look? Even frosted my tips."

"Terrific," Dantley said, but he was frowning. And his attention was already slipping away from her back to the car, *his* car. "Could we hurry up? Could you go a little faster, please?"

Chapter Ten

In the parking lot of the Flamingo, Wayne Lowry was meeting a prospective client. The man had been late, but Wayne hadn't minded waiting for him because he could tell from the blend of eagerness and greed in the man's voice when he had called for the appointment that he was almost certain to order a custom job from Silverado. Wayne knew the tone very well, and he smiled cynically when he had heard this man. "Listen," the man had said, "what I want to know most of all is, how can you do this work so cheap?"

"Low profit margin," Wayne had said. "Big turnover." He was being cautious. Sometimes he told customers that Silverado imported Mexican labor—*skilled* Mexican labor, mind you, but cheap.

"Okay," the man had said. "Flamingo parking lot at eleven. What do I look for?"

"Stingray," Wayne replied. "Red and orange. You can't miss it."

And so he had sat in the Stingray, waiting until 11:30, listening to some soft music on the tape deck, enjoying the glances and gazes that passersby directed at the car, some curious, some amazed, some envious. Wayne had come to anticipate such glances ever since he had driven the stolen car out of Monk's truck, and when they came he received them with only the slightest hint of an acknowledging smile. In the short time that he had been driving the car he had come to feel not only that he owned it, had acquired it legitimately, but had in fact been responsible for its splendid renovation.

Five years earlier, in high school, he had wanted to do such a fine custom job on a Corvette and he told himself that he *would* have done it, too, if he had had the time, if he had had the breaks, if other, more lucrative temptations had not come his way. His shop teacher had told him once that he was the most skilled and conscientious student he had ever taught, and that if he chose to do so he could raise car customizing to a fine art, setting standards and fashioning designs that would make Detroit sit up and take notice, just as George Barris and Ed Roth had done. And, in fact, Wayne had set out to do just that. But serious customizing was hard, lonely work that brought uncertain rewards; and he found with time that he needed money quickly, and then more money, and then, after a child and a divorce, a steady source of money for alimony and support. And so, bit by bit, his customizing business had become almost totally a front for the alteration of stolen cars. He was not quite sure how that had happened—he had talked about his financial troubles, old friends in the business of stealing cars had visited him, one car had led to another. The process had been so painless and effortless that even now it was a shock to him when he realized that he actually was a crook, that he had become a crook, and that almost all his income came from illegal activities. For a kid who had never learned what an equation was, or how to write a sentence, he had done well. Still, he was surprised some mornings when he looked in the mirror. The face was not what he expected; it was the face of a survivor. The eyes said, "I don't trust you!"; and it was only when they registered shock at themselves in the mirror that Wayne was able to glimpse something of the innocence and vulnerability that had once been his.

Usually when he drove the Corvette, even on rainy days, he wore sunglasses; then, when he caught a glimpse of himself in the broad rear-view mirror, he could maintain his illusion that he was still the kid who had wanted to build this car, and who had done so. For a little while, it was really his.

"Very nice. *Very* nice. I like your car very much." The client had interrupted Wayne's daydream, and was now standing stolid and unsmiling at the driver's door, sun glinting off his thick glasses and the clasps of his briefcase. He looked like a Nixon lawyer. "I assume you're Mr. Lowry. Could we talk now? I only have ten minutes."

"Certainly, Mr. Lobell." And smiling, Wayne stepped out of the Stingray and spread his sample books on the fender. "Now, I understand that you're interested in a recent-model Buick Riviera, is that right?"

"That's right. Black."

"Black. Of course. And modified to suit. Now here are a few possibilities Silverado can offer you. The front end for example . . ."

Within ten minutes all details had been decided upon, Wayne had accepted the customer's deposit in a thick brown envelope, and they had left in separate directions.

Dantley and Vanessa, driving in from the opposite end of the parking lot, missed glimpsing the unmistakable tail of the Stingray only by seconds. Dantley had ridden almost all the way with his hand on the door handle, ready to leap out and chase his car the instant he saw it, but when they had searched the lot he collapsed despondently back into his seat.

"It was here, Kenny. I swear it!" Vanessa pounded the steering wheel. Damn! Damn it!"

"Yeah. Well, it could be anywhere, now. You sure it was a right-hand drive?"

"Sure."

"Anybody in it?"

"Hey! Yeah! I meant to tell you that. There was a guy—for a minute I thought it was you because his hair was just about the same, you know? Only smoothed down. But then I saw the side of his face. Funny, though; he *did* look like you, only older."

Dantley beat a brisk, tense tattoo on his knees. "Well, at least it's still in Las Vegas. Thanks for trying."

She shrugged. "No problem. Now what?"

"Let's get out of here," Dantley said, peering distastefully at the hotel. "This is a terrible place. What're you doing around here, anyway?"

"I work here." She shrugged again. "So far, just in the beauty shop. But it's not bad. It really isn't. And it gives me a chance to watch people, and see how they dress and act, and . . ."

"Look, let's go someplace," Dantley said. "I'll buy you some lunch. Tell me about it then. Thing is, I really *hate* this place."

Ten minutes later, they were sitting at an umbrella-covered table, Dantley disconsolately munching french fries and watching the traffic pass, Vanessa chatting happily. "True," she was saying, "the salary's not much, but if they tip really good I'll be making two hundred a week. And the thing is, I'm *learning!* Wow, you should *see* some of those women"—she slapped his elbow—"I'm sitting there giving them a manicure, you know, and I'm looking at fifty carats of diamonds *on each hand!*"

Dantley shrugged. "What happened to your big-hooker number?"

"I'm learning, I'm learning."

"Sort of an apprenticeship."

"Right!"

"Look. Let me tell you something. You're not ever gonna be a prostitute. You just haven't got it, know what I mean?"

"You're right! *You are so right!* I have decided that I am not going to *be* a prostitute. In fact, there are no prostitutes in Las Vegas. But there are lots of *escorts*. And that is what I am in training to be, an escort."

"A whore by any other name," Dantley said, grinning sourly as he recalled the detestable Forrie Redman, jock and ex-Marine, droning the original poem.

"Names are important. As a matter of fact I've been thinking about Vanessa. That name has got to go. What do you think of . . . Rosalind?"

"Rosalind? What's wrong with Vanessa?"

"Well, it's not my real name anyway. My real name's Eleanor. And besides, I think it would be a mistake for me to keep it."

Dantley clutched his stomach and began to rise, eyes bulging.

"Okay, okay," she said, waving her hands. "How about Tiffany?"

"My car!" he shouted. "There's my car!"

"Where?"

"There!" And sure enough, there it was, gliding past in the center lane, the sun glinting, gleaming, glowing, and flashing on all its curves and angles.

Dantley's chair crashed to the pavement as he started to run. The french fries scattered in vinegar-sodden lumps across the tablecloth. As he rounded the corner onto the sidewalk, his hat flew off, and Vanessa had a brief and grimly silent tug-of-war with a passing Boston bulldog in order to retrieve it. Then, calmly sipping her milkshake, she crossed to her van and climbed in. "Support and consolation," she said to herself. "The eternal role of women." Her straw made a sound like a draining bathtub; she tossed the empty carton into a container within range of her window, and started the engine.

By the time she had slid into the curb beside him, Dantley had run three blocks. His eyes were bulging, his breathing sounded like an overworked sump pump, his feet were slapping the pavement like a clown's oversized shoes. And he was reaching out toward the Stingray, which even then was slowly but relentlessly eluding his grasp. "Wanna lift, fella?" She raised a Lauren Bacall eyebrow. Dantley fell into the passenger's seat, panting and pointing a desperate, wordless command: Follow that car!

"You seem to be using my wheels a lot," Vanessa said, accelerating cleanly and shifting from first to second. "When you goin to get your own?"

"Just go," Dantley spluttered. "Go!"

And she did. If he had been watching her performance, rather than the neat red-orange tail of his Corvette weaving through the traffic, Dantley would have had to admit that she drove superbly well. She drove even a *van* well. And by the second block it was clear that she was gaining on the Corvette. Then, just ahead, to Dantley's horror, a light began to change—green to yellow—the Corvette slipped through—and yellow to red. Vanessa stopped. "What're you doin'?" Dantley shrieked. "Tromp it, tromp it!" He stamped a brisk tattoo on the floorboards with both feet.

"I can't," she said, "It's illegal."

"Are you out of your mind?"

"It's a red light, dummy! See? Red!"

"Go through, damn it! That's my *car!*" The Corvette was receeding sedately, horribly, into the distance.

"It's illegal."

"Illegal! Hit it!" He reached over and crushed her small foot with his large one. The engine roared like an enraged tiger, but the van stayed where it was; Vanessa's left foot resolutely held the clutch down.

"Kenny!"

"Go! Go!"

"Kenny, you're hurting my foot . . ."

"Please! You're gonna lose him."

" . . . It hurts, Kenny. And besides, there's someone over here"—her eyes swirled leftward—"who's very interested in your performance."

Dantley looked past her, into the cool, visored gazes of two police officers in their cruiser. In the same instant the light turned green and Vanessa began to pull ahead. "Stop! Stop!" Arms waving furiously, Dantley lept from the van and ran in front of it and the cruiser. "Stolen car! Stolen car!"

Cautiously, the officers emerged. "Pills disagree with you, son?"

"What? No! No pills! My car, see"—he waved toward the fast-diminishing dot of color that was the Corvette—"stolen! We have time to catch it."

"What kind of car is that, son?"

"Corvette."

"I see." The policemen nodded, lips pursed. "Corvette Stingray. And you claim it's yours?"

"It *is* mine!" Dantley rummaged frantically in his wallet and produced a newspaper clipping—a photograph of the Corvette and the class, himself driving, Kootz hanging over the bumper grinning inanely, and all the others. The patrolmen peered shrewdly at this, as did Vanessa, who had dropped down from the van and who stood on tiptoe to peer between their shoulders.

"Hey!" she exclaimed. "Hey, Kenny, this isn't even your car. You've been shitting me, Kenny! This is the *school's* car!" She suddenly began to pound the shoulders of the policeman. "It's the *school's* car!"

"It's mine!" Dantley shouted. "I built it! But what's it matter; it's stolen, isn't it? And he's getting away with it!"

"C'mon, son." One of the policemen pushed back his cap and took Dantley's arm. "Come and sit down. We'll make a call about that car, okay? Radio's faster than rubber, right? You just give us the license number, okay?"

Dantley looked blank, defeated. "I didn't notice," he said.

"Nevada PRB23," Vanessa said, shrugging off the surprised and grateful glance Dantley gave her.

The younger cop spoke some numbers into the radio and then waited, microphone in hand, while the radio made gentle frying sounds. Then an anonymous woman's voice came back to them: "On your vehicle

I.D. check, stolen Nevada PRB23, we show no such Nevada registration. Repeat, no such Nevada registration."

Again the cop spoke some numbers and hung up the microphone. He turned to Dantley. "Sorry, kid."

"He forged it! It's a phony plate!"

"Maybe. Look, kid, why don't you and your girlfriend here just go somewhere and have a good night's sleep. We'll keep an eye out for the car, okay?"

Dantley pounded his palm and danced in frustration. "You won't! First of all, you don't believe me, and second of all you just don't give a shit!"

"Look, kid . . ."

"*I'll* find it," Dantley said, pointing. "You wait and see if I don't!"

"C'mon," Vanessa said, putting her arm around his shoulders. "Come on home."

She thought afterwards that that was a very strange thing for her to say. She had never said that to anyone before, and she could not remember anyone's having said it to her. "Home" in her experience was something that you talked about as little as possible and got away from as soon as possible; and she could not imagine why she had thought the word might comfort Kenny Dantley at that moment, or what she had intended. She *was* home. She drove home around wherever she wanted. And she knew that for Dantley too, home had always been on wheels, ready to roll away at any moment.

But she had said this, made this invitation, and he had acquiesced and was now slouched disconsolately in the passenger's seat while she drove; and she guessed, shrugging, that what she had meant was that she had to decide where home was going to be parked that night.

She chose a distant, darkening corner of a shopping plaza in the farthest outskirts of the city, and she parked so that the whole glittering, glowing, pulsating skyline of Las Vegas was obscured by the paneling of the van, and so that all they could see through the windshield and the two oblong windows on the left side was the first scattering of stars appearing in the dark purple of the evening sky, and the deeper blue and amber that was the desert and the hills on the far horizon.

When she stopped the engine, everything was incredibly quiet; neither of them could recall ever before experiencing an evening that was not torn by accelerating engines and gnawed by whining transmissions. Dantley sat up, and blinked, and resettled his cap on his head, and peered through the window at the desert. "Quiet," he said.

"Mmm."

"No lights," he said. "As far as you can see, no lights. Except those over there."

"Those aren't lights, dummy. They're stars."

"Oh, yeah."

"You scared?" She asked after a minute.

"What of?"

"I dunno. Just . . . of *nothing*."

He shook his head. "Naw. It's *people* you want to be scared of, not this." Far away an animal—perhaps a dog, perhaps a coyote—began a long, low, mournful howling that continued for half a minute, then stopped. They listened. "As a matter of fact," Dantley said, "I wouldn't mind going for a walk."

"Walk?"

"Yeah. You know, one foot in front of the other?"

"Where? Where do you want to go? We can drive."

"I don't want to go anywhere in particular. Just out there a little way."

"Okay," she said, hesitantly. And they got out their respective doors, both feeling that the flash of the automatic roof light was an intrusion on their privacy, and both closing the doors as quietly as possible. They walked down a slight embankment littered with the usual refuse of the plaza—cartons, cans, butts, and greasy, anonymous crumpled scraps of paper—an occasional bottle—but almost immediately they had left this behind and they were in the desert, feeling the uncertainty of sand under their feet and gawking up like kids at the great star-filled bowl that was the heavens. Neither was quite certain how it happened, but almost in the same instant they became aware that they had been holding hands for some time. Boy, Dantley thought, is that dumb. Is that ever *dumb!* But he did not let go.

It was cool, and calm, and very soothing. His obsession, the car, retreated for the time being to the farthest edges of his consciousness; he was scarcely aware of it, and when he thought of it at all it was not as something lost but as something misplaced. The notion crossed his mind that when he got back to the van he would write to Mr. McGrath just to keep in touch and to let him know that he had seen the car and that he would, still, repossess it and return it. But then he realized with a kind of relief, and fear also, that he had no writing paper, not even a postcard, and so the correspondence would have to wait until morning.

So he had no excuse when Vanessa, shivering a little in the cold, stood on her tiptoes and whispered, "Let's go home now," so close to his ear that she was almost kissing him.

"Sure," he said. "Why not." And he put his arm around her.

Later, they lay together on the vast waterbed, gazing out through the oblong windows at the incredible vistas offered by the late-rising, waning moon on the desert.

"There," she said, running a finger down the center of his chest, "That wasn't so bad, was it"

"Bad!" He laughed. "It was neat."

"Neat! Come on, I know you're no Shakespeare, but you can do better than that, can't you? Neat! Zheesh!"

"I mean, well it was incredible! Wonderful!"

"Better."

"You know, it was almost even better than . . ." He hesitated.

"Than what?"

"Well, than driving the car."

"Hey. That *is* something."

"What I can't understand is why, when I drove my first car at nine, and overhauled my first transmission when I was ten, and turned a quarter-mile under twelve seconds when I was thirteen, why did I wait until eighteen to have *this* experience? Why?"

"You were scared," she said.

"Ha!"

"No, you were. Listen," she pushed herself up on an elbow so she could see his face, "if we're gonna spend any time together, we gotta get in the habit of telling the truth, okay? I know it's not easy. It's not even easy to *see* it sometimes, and that's why, when you do see it, you gotta tell it. Okay?"

"Yeah," Dantley said. "Okay. I was scared."

"And now?"

"I'm not so scared anymore."

After a very profitable evening on the Strip, Wayne Lowry had run the Corvette out through the outskirts of town, out through North Vegas, past the drive-in restaurants and service stations and the low regions of modest signs where Vegas became indistinguishable from the bland anonymity of a thousand other North American cities, until he had passed the last corner of the last shopping plaza, where a Dodge van, richly red and white, sat parked in the shadows facing the desert. Then he was in the desert himself, and the Stingray's four big rectangular headlights were sweeping across a moonlit landscape that was as flat and clear as the highway. He accelerated smoothly to one hundred and ten miles an hour, listening carefully all the way to the responses of the machine, and enjoying the lazy ease with which it met his demands. Again, as he had many times since the car had fallen into his possession, he admired the skill and dedication which had brought it into being, and his admiration was soured by envy and regret.

In the early hours of the morning he returned to Silverado and parked the car safely behind a reinforced garage door that swung openly automatically to receive him, and dropped shut automatically behind him. Before switching off the light, he turned for one last look at the machine and—the result of too much tension and bourbon and fatigue—saw a flickering image of his auto-shop teacher telling him, as he had told him often in that last year of high school, his left eye twitching in that way that had always fascinated Wayne, that he had the talent—the "gift"—he had called it, to become a true stylist, an artist in automotive design. Had anyone been watching at that moment they would have seen Wayne's face soften into that of a man capable once again of dreams; but then, almost instantly, it hardened. He dismissed the memory with a wave and a disparaging grunt, and made his way upstairs, alone, to the lavishly decorated apartment he kept above the shop where he remodeled stolen cars.

Chapter Eleven

Two days later, Ed McGrath got a card from Dantley. On one side was a photograph of a half-nude, plastic-looking showgirl. On the other side was this message:

Dear Mr. McGrath: Here I am still in Las Vegas surrounded by beauty ha ha. But seriously I am here because I have see our car again and am tracking it down and will bring it back as promised so don't worry. Everything is fine with me and I hope everything is fine with you and that you are enjoying summer school ha ha.

Kenny

When he had taken this card from his mailbox and read it, McGrath tapped the edge of it absentmindedly against his thigh as he returned up the driveway to his house. His home was a sprawling ranch-style bungalow with fruit trees on the groomed front lawn and children laughing in a pool at the back. Sometimes, looking at this home that represented the fulfillment of a long-time dream, Ed McGrath wondered why he felt so deprived, so failed, so *sad*. And he wondered why he worried so much. "Jesus Christ, Ed," Forrie Redman had said to him once, "why is it that you look go goddamn *worried*? After all, you've arrived, haven't you? You've really got it made, haven't you?" And he had shrugged and smiled wanly, and said yes, he guessed so, but there was something . . . something . . .

If the truth was told, Ed McGrath never for an instant had felt that he had arrived anywhere. Despite the house, and the family, and the substantial bank account, he still felt that he was on the move and vulnerable. Worry had put bags under his eyes, and trimmed his mouth to a tight line, and notched heavy creases into his pudgy cheeks from nose to jowl, and arched his eyebrows into wispy tepees, and etched deep, parallel, vertical lines through the lower half of his forehead. Even in deep shade, even at night, he seemed to be squinting against strong sunlight. Night and day he suffered with the spasmodic tic in his left eye. He was a chronically worried man; in the same way that some people enjoy bad health, Ed McGrath enjoyed concern.

Not that he had nothing to worry him. Here was this kid, this Dantley, innocently, aggressively on the verge of doing them both serious injury, and he was very much aware, as he strolled back through the front door of the house that Saturday morning, that some action had to be taken. By the time he had reached the kitchen he had decided what it would be.

"Goin' down to the school for awhile," he said to his wife.

He did go to the school, although only long enough to find an address in the records of the main office. When he drove to that address—a trailer park in the north end—he arrived just in time to catch Dantley's mother in the midst of moving. There was a black LTD, making a sound which he recognized instantly as a defective water pump, backing up to the Dantley trailer, and there was a woman in her early forties, with her looks more or less intact, giving instructions to the driver of the LTD, a gentleman with rich, black, and somewhat oily hair.

"Another four inches," she was saying, indicating the space with her thumb and forefinger. "Four, two, that's it!"

"Excuse me," McGrath said, "but my name is Ed McGrath? I'm Kenny's autoshop teacher at school—at

101

least I was?" He didn't know why he was tipping these statements into questions. His whole expression and posture emanated a paternal concern.

"Hi," she said. "Kenny's teacher," she said to Borodino, who had begun to connect the trailer hitch. Borodino nodded without pausing. "What's wrong?" she asked. "Kenny in trouble?"

"No. I don't think so. That is, not exactly. But I'd like to get in touch with him on a school matter, and I wondered if you had an address."

"Address." She shrugged and looked blank. "Vegas is all I know."

"He hasn't written?"

She shook her head and there was a sudden quivering in her lower lip that came and went so quickly that McGrath could not even be certain he had seen it. "He's an independent kid, you know? I raised him to be independent. Hold on a minute." She opened the car door and began to rummage for something in the back seat. Borodino, meanwhile, had been busy methodically disconnecting the trailer's water, electrical, and sewage hookups, and taking off the flimsy aluminum side panels to reveal wheels, which he routinely kicked. "Ready to go," he said to Kenny's mother as she returned, and he got into the car and started it.

"When you see him," she said to McGrath, "will you tell him where I've gone? And would you give him these, please?"

"Where *have* you gone?"

"Del Mar," she said. "Somewhere in Del Mar, tell him."

McGrath waved two fingers—okay—and watched the mobile home towed ponderously away down the gravel road of the trailer camp and out onto the highway. Only after they had gone and he was returning to his own car did he actually look at what she had given him. It was a collection of loose pictures, some with thumbtack holes in the corners and some with bits of scotch tape still adhering, all obviously taken off a wall.

Most were cars, and most of the cars were Corvettes, but there were a few pictures, yellowing and badly out of focus, of a smiling and confident-looking young man in the clothing and brush cut of the late fifties. A Corvette also appeared in these photographs, sometimes so prominently that it seemed that the photographer was unsure of the true subject of the shot—man or car.

"Oh, God," McGrath said, settling himself heavily behind the steering wheel and placing the collection on the seat beside him, "she might at least have put them in an envelope!"

"Thanks," Forrie Redman said, taking the envelope from McGrath and tucking it into the inside pocket of his jacket. He handled both envelope and the jacket with his fingertips to avoid smearing them with sweat. Sweat streamed down his face and neck and spread in a dark stain across the chest of his T-shirt. Outside the locker room the teachers' Saturday-afternoon basketball game raced ahead at full speed, full of shouts and the sounds of rubber soles, slapping, squeaking, and thumping on hardwood. Once, a breathless, distant voice shouted, "Hurry up, Forrie, we need you!"

"How'd it go?" McGrath asked.

Redman made a thumb and finger circle. "Piece of cake."

"No problems?"

"No problems, Ed." Laughing, Redman shook the older man's shoulders. "Jeez! Why are you always looking for problems? You *like* problems? I tell you, there was nothing to it. There it was, a nice seventy-six Buick Riviera, just like the man ordered, sitting there with the keys in the ignition. I got in and"—he brushed his palms together—"drove away."

"Is it loaded?"

"Loaded and sent in the usual fashion. And right at this instant, knowing the way Monk hoofs that semi along, it's halfway to Vegas. Don't *worry*, Ed!"

103

"I can't help worrying. When you got problems you worry, right? And we got a problem."

"What?"

"Dantley."

"Kenny Dantley? The kid who was here last year? What about him?"

"He's tracked down the Stingray. He's in Vegas."

"What!"

"I don't think he's tracked it to Wayne, yet, but it's only a matter of time." McGrath slapped the wall of the dressing room. "I should have *known*. We shouldn't have picked that car, Forrie. Any car but that one."

"Okay. So what do we do now? Can we get the kid back?"

McGrath shrugged. "Can't even find him. All I get are these postcards now and again." He showed Redman the newest Dantley correspondence.

"God," said Redman, reading, "Look at his punctuation! Look at his spelling! We let this kid *graduate?*"

"That's beside the point, isn't it?"

"Standards are slipping, Ed. There's no question about it. Jeez, look at this! The kid's an illiterate."

"Maybe." McGrath tapped a finger on Redman's sweaty chest, his eye twitching frantically. "But he's an illiterate who can blow the whistle on us. And he's also, incidentally, an illiterate that I'm rather fond of and don't want to see get hurt!"

For a moment the two men looked at each other in silence. Outside, the cheerful basketball game raged on.

"Okay," Redman said, "so here's what we do. If we can't get to the kid we get to Wayne. And we tell him he's got to get rid of the car—ship it to Denver. He's got no alternative, right?"

"Right."

"You call," Redman said. "I gotta go play basketball."

And so McGrath, looking more worried than ever,

left by the outside door and drove home where, in the privacy of his study, he called Wayne.

"Get *rid* of it!" Wayne's shout hurt McGrath's ear. "Why the hell should I get rid of it?"

"Well there's a kid looking for it." McGrath shrugged deferentially as he spoke, realizing how ridiculous this must sound at the other end. "He's a very determined kid. He's seen the car, knows it's there and, well, the chances are that he'll track it down to you if you hold onto it."

"A *kid*! And I'm supposed not to be able to handle a kid?"

"Look," McGrath realized that a note of pleading had entered his voice in spite of his efforts to maintain control, and that a thin film of perspiration had coated his brow and his upper lip—a film he was thankful that Wayne couldn't see. "Why take that chance? Our agreement was when we started that nobody was gonna get hurt, remember? It was gonna be clean and *harmless*." He hadn't meant to shout, but a memory had returned to him so abruptly that it struck like a blow in the solar plexus—an image that he had forgotten—of Wayne as a student, angered by something a younger boy had said or done in the shop, holding a jack handle, as if it were a pistol, under the other boy's chin and backing him up, step by slow tiptoed step, in silence, with a look in his eye that made even McGrath, although he was much trimmer and younger then, hesitate to interfere.

Wayne said nothing for a moment, and when he did speak his voice was softer, and slower, and much more terrifying. "And you're forgetting the other part of our agreement . . ."

"I haven't for—"

". . . which was that you would look after your end and I would look after mine."

"Yes, but—"

"This kid is at my end, Ed. Not yours. And I'll look

after him in my own way if he comes snooping around."

"But—"

"*My* way, Ed. But please don't phone up here and tell me to get rid of this Corvette, because I have no intention of doing so, not with the kind of business it's bringing in. That would just not be wise, Ed. Just not good business. You follow?"

"Yeah. Okay." McGrath looked around him like a man trapped—at his paneled study, at his children splashing in their pool, at his car gleaming in the driveway.

"Good boy. By the way, did you and Forrie get that Riviera for me?"

"Yeah. It's on its way, Monk's bringing it down."

"Good. And there's some money on its way to *you*, Ed, my friend. Quite a bit of money this month, as a matter of fact—enough to make me think that maybe we should review our percentages. Anyway, we'll be in touch. You take care now, y'hear? And don't worry about any *kid*, for godsake."

The line droned. McGrath settled the phone back into its cradle. "Yeah," he said. "Okay." The creases in his forehead and along the sides of his mouth had deepened appreciably, and the nervous tick in his left eye had become almost continuous.

Within a day, Dantley had found another job, and it was, of course, a job that would give him ample opportunity to keep a watchful eye on the traffic of Las Vegas. He was washing cars; rather, he was drying them after the automatic sprayers, roll-towelers, waxers, and air driers had all done their work. He wore orange overalls with someone else's name—Sam—stitched above his left breast, and his responsibility was to dry completely, every last drop that might have escaped the blow-drier, the left side of a car while Willie, a lanky black who whistled. hummed, and composed variations on "Yankee Doodle" for the entire day, dried the right side. Dantley didn't care about any of this; it was a job, it paid enough to buy food for Vanessa and himself, and he was outside where he could watch the road as well as the cars coming through the wash. "Sooner or later," he kept thinking "Sooner or later . . ."

Every day at 4:30, quitting time, he began to make his rounds of garages, automotive suppliers, body shops, and other establishments where the Stingray might have appeared and been remembered. One by one he talked to the proprietors and showed them his remaining copy of the newspaper photo taken, it seemed to him, decades earlier. One by one he got sympathetic shrugs and shakes of the head, and one by one he crossed them off the list he had compiled from the yellow pages, until, by the fourth day, he found that he was working mainly in the outskirts of Las Vegas, and often behind the bleak, blistered tin walls of the body shops he caught glimpses of the desert itself.

So it was that he came on the evening of the fifth day, to Silverado Auto Body & Paint "Special Cars for Special People." And it so happened that when he arrived there he found, not his Stingray, which was sitting just barely out of sight at the rear of the shop, but a gorgeous, gleaming black Trans Am, so beautiful that for an instant he forgot his own car in the sheer joy of seeing something so well done. There was a man kneeling in the last rays of the sun, Polaroid glasses pushed up into his hair, absorbed in taking photos of the Trans Am with a glinting Nikon, and Dantley felt a shock of recognition, so strongly did the man's posture, and carriage, and demeanor remind him of the other young man, the one he had never really known but of whom he had pictures, leaning in his 1957 T-shirt and jeans against the fender of a Corvette convertible.

"Yeah," said Wayne, catching sight of him and straightening up. "Can I help you?"

Dantley looked at him only long enough to realize

107

two things: that he was not the man in the Fifties picture, and that he did not like him. It was, in fact, more than dislike that he felt; it was distrust. He turned his attention to the car. "Nice," he said, "Mighty nice."

"You like that?"

"I'll say." Dantley ran his finger along the edge of the fender "What've you got on there, Kitten Wax?"

Wayne stood up and folded the case around his Nikon. "That's right. Twelve coats of color rubbed out with Ditzler DRX-55."

Dantley nodded. "And what's cookin' in there?"

Smiling, Wayne swung the hood up. "A '68 396 bored out to 402. TRW pistons, L-88 rods, Sig Erson cam, and an 800 Holley."

Dantley gave a low whistle. "You got the Muncie four-speed?"

"Reprogrammed hydro. Listen, kid, what can I do for you?"

The word stung like a bee. Kid! They had been talking man to man, equals in understanding and in their appreciation of taste and craftsmanship, and now, with one word, this man had reasserted the space between the man who rode and the boy who walked. No, Dantley decided, he definitely did not like this person.

"Car," he said, drawing out the photograph which he had enclosed in a protective fold of plexiglass. "I'm looking for this car. Wonder if you've seen it."

Wayne held the photograph a moment, looking at it very hard. Then he drew his sunglasses back down over his eyes and shrugged. "A very nice machine," he said. "I certainly would remember it if I'd seen it, which I haven't. Yours?"

"Sure, mine." Dantley said. He rubbed his nose with the back of his hand. "Stolen."

"Too bad, kid." Wayne was smiling.

"For *them*, that's all," Dantley said. "It's here. In Vegas. I'm gonna find it. Thanks." He took the picture and started to walk away.

"Hey, kid." Dantley kept walking. "Kid. Listen. You

want to be careful, you know what I mean? You run up against whoever ripped off that Stingray and you're liable to get yourself a bloody nose."

"I'll remember that," Dantley said.

"A bloody nose, or worse."

Dantley kept walking, tossing a wave of the merest acknowledgment over one shoulder, and Wayne watched him go, smiling in a way that was no longer even remotely pleasant. Then he turned and went into the shop, where Jeff was on his back under a car, his face grease-smeared and pale green in the light of a naked bulb. "Hey," Wayne tapped his foot with a toe. "Drop whatever you're doing and bring the Corvette in. We're gonna paint it."

Dantley hitchhiked back to the edge of the parking lot where he and Vanessa had left the van. He walked the last mile across its deserted expanse of asphalt. It was late evening, and the last of the red clouds had strung themselves out like a crumpled, bloody bandage along the western horizon. Except for a laughing group of thirteen-year-olds on mopeds, chasing a cat, there was no one else in sight. When he reached it, he checked around the van to make sure that no tires were flat and that all hubcaps were in place, and amazingly, he found that it had not been tampered with. But under the windshield wiper fluttered a scrap of paper; he tugged it out and read it. "Working," it said. "Back late."

For a moment Dantley puzzled over this. He knew that the beauty shop closed at five, but he knew—although he did not own a watch—that it was now almost ten, and where could she . . . Then it hit him. Working! It hit him in a series of visible images— Vanessa indolently drinking her milkshake through a straw, talking about changing her name, Vanessa talking about "escorts" and women with fingers encrusted with diamonds, Vanessa . . .

He was driving before he realized it, with no idea

109

where he was going, except that the van was swinging in a broad circle, tires squealing, away from the desert and toward the lights of the city. He knew that wherever she had gone she had walked unless—and this thought made his stomach contract—someone had picked her up! He refused to think about that; he refused to imagine a smooth, powerful machine, perhaps a Corvette, drawing up to the curb beside her, and Vanessa stepping in. Rather, he preferred to imagine her still walking—and he drove slowly, examining carefully the strolling women on both sides of the street. Rather, he preferred to imagine her even then enlisting in some "Escort" service. And in the same instant that the word crossed his mind it appeared in front of his eyes, in green and blue fluorescent—"Good Company Escort Service."

He was out of the van and inside before he had really thought about what he was doing ("Dantley," McGrath had said to him once, "the problem with some people is that their mouths move ahead of their minds. With you it's different: your *feet* move and your mind follows!" The class had laughed. "Implosive, right, Mr. McGrath?" "Impulsive, Kootz," Dantley had replied. "You twit.") And he was impulsive. Tattered cap brim low over his eyes and jaw thrust forward, he was past the silver-haired receptionist even before he saw her, even before it had registered on him that she was trotting along behind, wagging a pencil at him and saying, "Hey, hey there, honey, where do you think you're going?" The fact was that he wasn't thinking at all, but he knew where he was going—through the door and into the back room where a half-dozen girls looked up at him expectantly from where they lounged, waiting, on various chairs and couches. He recognized only one, and she had her back turned to him in what seemed to Dantley a pathetic attempt to avoid him. In two strides he was across the room and seizing her, swinging her around, saying, "Listen. You know, you make me . . ." But the face that was turned to him was not Vanessa's, clean and smiling, but the seamed and pitted one of some thirty-year-old floozy who had managed somehow to keep her figure. Shocked, Dantley recoiled and would have apologized, except that in that instant he himself was seized, seized very forcibly by both shoulders, spun around, and lifted clean off his feet by a huge Samoan in a Panama hat and zebra scarf. The Samoan smelled of Eau Sauvage and peppermint. His face was so gleaming smooth that it reflected the lights of the room, and his voice was the whisper of dangerous insects. "Now, now, now," he said. "What have we here, hm? Little fella. Little fella likes it rough does he, eh? Rough and tough?" And while he spoke, he was carrying Dantley down the hall, past the smug receptionist, and to the door, and he was backing him through the door and onto the street.

When they got there, he very gently turned Dantley's cap around, catcher-style, and then he asked, "This your van, hm? This yours? Your van?" And he kept asking despite the fact that Dantley kept nodding, until they were right beside it. "My, what a nice, nice van." And then, to Dantley's horror, still smiling, the Samoan reached out with one hamlike fist and crushed the rear-view mirror on the passenger's door into a tangled, wretched mess of metal and glass. Then, very gently, he patted Dantley on the head, dropped the mirror into the gutter as casually as anyone else might drop a squashed bug, and returned toward the door.

Dantley climbed into the van, started the engine, shouted through the opened passenger's window, "Find a tree, ya goddamn gorilla!" He drove many blocks before he stopped shaking, and several more before he remembered that his cap was twisted around. In fact, he was almost there before the fact registered on him that he was going home, to the parking lot. He was less than half a mile away when he realized this, and at the same time he realized that he was ravenously hungry. He entered the first drive-in he came to. "Burger, fries, Coke," he said into the intercom, and when he had re-

111

ceived no acknowledgement except static and the rattle of dishes in the background, he added, "Got that?"

"Hi. Kenny?" the speaker said.

Dantley started and stared suspiciously at the box. "Whosat?"

"It's *me*, dummy." There was a tinkle of laughter. "Vanessa!"

But before he had even heard the name, he knew. And he was out of the van and running toward the brightly lit little box at the end of the parking lot. "What are you *doing* here?" he shouted, bursting in. "God, I've been looking all *over* for you! What are you doing here?"

"Working, obviously. "Didn't you get my note? It's Friday night. I work late, Fridays."

"What happened to the beauty parlor?"

"Quit."

"Quit, why?"

She brushed back a strand of hair from her forehead and put down the spatula that she was using to flip the hamburg patties sizzling on the grill. "Why do *you* think?"

"I don't know. We didn't discuss it."

"Discuss it! My God, who do you think you are, my *husband?* Do you think you own me, for godsake? If you think I'm going to talk over everything with you before or after I do it, you're out of your tree! And you can go find yourself another van."

For several moments Dantley stared at her, saying nothing, while she angrily squashed and prodded the hamburg patties. The little kitchen was filled with the cooking sounds and with the demands of arriving customers—"Fries . . . two Cokes . . . onion rings . . ."—which the other girl on duty, a scrawny, pimply blond, tried desperately to fill.

Then he said, "I'm sorry. I was just worried about you."

She glanced at him, shrugged, and grinned. She brushed back the strand of hair again and, in doing so,

112

brushed the corner of her eye. "Worried. Gee, I don't think anybody's ever *worried* about me before. My old man sure wasn't worried about me."

"I thought you told me . . ."

"That he was a really religious and concerned parent. Yeah. I tell everybody that at first. I can make it funny, you know, about getting kicked out and everything. But that's not quite the way it was. Not *quite*." She prodded at the meat. "Sometime I'll tell you. Sometime. Not now."

". . . Three super cheeseburgers . . . three root beers . . ."

"Anyway," Dantley said, "What time will you be home?"

She smiled, came over to him, hugged him. She smelled of grease smoke and her cheek tasted salty. "Eleven," she said. "I'm through at eleven."

He started to leave.

"By the way," she added, "I haven't answered your question. I left the beauty shop because I wasn't seeing enough cars. That's all changed." She indicated the endless traffic visible through the window, and the lineup along the curb, waiting to be served. "I decided that if we're looking for something really important, two sets of eyes are better than one."

"Thanks," Dantley said. He adjusted his cap before he closed the door. "See you."

Chapter Twelve

He did not tell Vanessa, but it had become very important to him not only to find the car, but now to find the car before she did. He did not know why this was so; certainly he was grateful for her help, but there was a deep, large part of him that wanted to do this on his own, having come this far, without help from anyone—McGrath, the police, Vanessa, anyone. And there was also a part of him, a troubling part, that especially did not want to be indebted to Vanessa—at least not *that* indebted.

As things turned out, he need not have worried, because it was he himself who was destined to find the car; rather, the car was destined to return to him. For it did, literally, return, and at a moment when Dantley was least expecting it. Later, he could not recall what he had been thinking about at that moment. The shock of looking up and seeing his machine moving toward him slowly, hazily, as in a dream, was so great that it seemed to have erased that little portion of his memory. There it was, hooked to the conveyor chain and passing through liquid screens that blurred and exaggerated its contours. He knew it instantly, despite the dreamlike distortions of the spraying water, and despite the fact that it was now a brilliant metallic gold. He stopped breathing. Sweat began to bead across his upper lip and in the small of his back. He couldn't move. Without turning his head, he glanced down the line of customers waiting for their cars, but could see no one who might have brought in the Stingray. The car came closer, passed through the wax, passed through the blowers. Snapping his towel, whistling "Yankee Doodle," Willie slipped into the driver's seat on the right side and began to work over the steering wheel, the dash, the rear-view mirror.

Probably it was simply the sight of someone else behind the wheel of his car that galvanized Dantley into action. He moved. He caught the door, swung it open, and touched Willie on the shoulder. "Out, brother."

"No, no, man. I feel a big tip comin'." Willie grinned.

Dantley gripped tighter, leaned closer. "You asshole. Get the hell outta this car. I'm taking it!" And bracing his foot against the rocker panel, adrenalin darting through all veins and arteries, he pulled and pivoted, lifting Willie bodily out of the seat. For an instant they stared at each other, eyeball to eyeball, frozen in a bizarre wrestlers' grip while the car inched relentlessly past them both; and if Jeff at that instant had not emerged from paying for his wash and dropped into the driver's seat, preparing to take off, the car might have eluded Dantley yet again, engaged as he would probably have been in a vigorous physical exchange with the black youth. But Jeff did get into the Stingray, making the mistake of rolling down the window at the same time. Euphoric now with rage and triumph, Dantley dropped the black youth and, reaching through the opened window, seized a fistful of Jeff's shirt just under the adam's apple. "You stole it," he said.

There was no mistaking the mingled shock and fright in Jeff's eyes for a split second before his expression turned sour, turned vicious. "Take your goddamn hands off me," he said, and slammed the car into gear.

But Dantley hung on. He skidded fifty feet across the asphalt, shoes smoking, before Jeff realized the hopelessness of trying to shake him off in that way, and stopped. They pushed and punched breathlessly and ineffectively at each other, muttering curses. By now, people were running to them—the other wipers, the attendants at the pumps out front, and farther back, the manager.

"Hey, man. Be cool!" Willie said, patting Dantley on both shoulders as if he sought to comfort him.

"Help me!" Dantley grunted, flailing away furiously at Jeff's head and shoulders. "This is my car! This sonuvabitch stole it!"

"Leggo of me!" Jeff was shouting, trying to protect himself and at the same time strike through the window at Dantley's midriff. "Man, you are *crazy!*"

"I know my own car, you bastard! And this it it! And you stole it!"

"Break it up," the manager said, seizing Dantley's belt and leaning back. The manager weighed 270 pounds, and although much of that was fat and concentrated toward his middle, nevertheless his grip had authority. Dantley bent into a U, hands furiously clawing at Jeff, who was by now several inches beyond reach.

"You hire maniacs?" Jeff asked the manager. "Don't you realize somebody could get hurt?" He was reaching inside his jacket pocket for his wallet. "Listen, do you take full responsibility for this person's actions?"

The manager hesitated, still holding on to Dantley's belt.

"I mean," Jeff went on, climbing out of the car and straightening his clothes, "for any damage to the car he might have caused? And, of course, for any personal injury?"

"That's my car," Dantley shouted hoarsely. "Mine! Don't believe him. Look at that paint. It's new! And that license number—PRB23—it doesn't *exist!* Look!" He extracted the newspaper of the car from his shirt pocket. "There it is. And that's *me!*"

"Registration," Jeff said, presenting his opened wallet for the manager's viewing while he inspected the

Stingray door for scratches. "Seems to be a little dent there. Hey," he said to Willie, "can you see that dent from where you're standing?"

"Phony!" Dantley shouted. "Fraud! Thief!" He was so furious that he was slobbering over his chin.

"You oughtta be locked up, fella" Jeff said, tapping his shirt front, "you're *dangerous!*"

"Wayne Lowry?" The manager inquired, squinting at the registration.

"That's right," Jeff said.

"Look, I'm very sorry about the inconvenience, Mr. Lowry. Please take this book of wash tickets free."

"So long, Dantley," said Willie, softly, making flying movements with his arms.

"You know how it is, Mr. Lowry," the manager continued. "Just impossible to get good help anymore. Kids irresponsible, drunked up, drugged up. Totally unreliable."

Jeff pocketed his wallet, stepped into the Stingray, and shut the door. "I know how it is," he said. "I'm in business myself."

"I guarantee it won't happen again, Mr. Lowry."

Jeff raised a hand, and in one easy motion the car left the lot and entered the stream of traffic.

"You bastards! You *gave* it to him!" Dantley shook himself free and started to run. Once again he ran blindly, unaware of the people in his path unaware of stop lights, unaware of everything except that bright red rear end casually, effortlessly, insultingly, once again receding from him. And once again he knew the hopelessness of the man on foot, the man who was certain to lose.

In his despair he began to try to flag down passing cars and trucks, shouting "Stolen car! Stolen!" but they swerved past him, waved him back, kept going. And then, curving around the next corner ahead, came a sight that brought a surge of joy to Dantley's heart—a bicyclist! And a beautiful, fast, ten-speed machine. At the last minute he danced out from between the parked

117

cars where he had crouched waiting, and the bicyclist couldn't possibly miss him. Down they went in a tangle of arms, legs, and chrome. "Jeez," the bicyclist said, sitting up groggily, "sorry, Mac. You okay?"

"Sure," Dantley said. "My fault. Gotta borrow this. Real important." And before the bicyclist was fully aware of what was happening, he had picked up the bicycle and wobbled off, perched on the too-high seat and struggling to find the toe-clips. "Gotta catch a thief," he shouted back.

"*You* gotta catch a thief . . . !" The bicycle owner struggled to his feet. "*Wait* a minute!"

Ahead, Jeff had pulled leisurely up to a stoplight, and was in the process of lighting a cigarette when he caught a glimpse in the rear-view mirror of a brilliant blob of orange approaching quickly. The blob was shouting and waving an arm. The kid from the car-wash! On a bike! Jeff glanced both ways and then ran the light, leaving neat rectangles of rubber where the wheels had been sitting. By the time Dantley reached it the light had turned green, and he went through it just as a huge mobile home lumbered past, proffering a beautiful, tubular roof ladder. Dantley swerved out, reached just as the ladder drew abreast of him, and hung on. Instantly he accelerated from fifteen to thirty. His arm felt wrenched out of its socket. The wind whipped tears from his eyes. The bike tires whined on the pavement like crazed insects. And in the next few blocks, which led straight through the suburbs and were free of all stoplights, the driver of the mobile home speeded up. Dantley hung on grimly. Through the blur of dust and tears he could see the rear end of the Stingray, and he knew that it was no longer pulling away from him; he was gaining on it!

Then to his horror, he realized that the Stingray was signaling a left turn, and the driver of the land yacht was swinging out to pass on the right. He let go, braked, swung behind the land yacht, past the noses of two astonished children and a woman who were

118

playing monopoly at the rear picture window, and crossed the traffic, going at least thirty-five miles an hour. Horns blared, people shouted. Dantley was oblivious to all of that, aware only that the Stingray was once again ahead of him, and that a beer truck, with a conveniently open side door, was lumbering up beside him. Again he grabbed, and hung on. Again he was whisked away at alarming speed, and this time he gained very rapidly on the Stingray.

Inside the Corvette, Jeff had checked the rear-view mirror before turning, just to make absolutely sure that the kid from the car wash was no longer following, and after he had turned, he checked once again. There was nothing behind but a beer truck. He slowed down, and tried again to light the cigarette he so badly wanted. His hand was shaking so badly that he could not find the end of the cigarette with the lighter, and he was steadying his hand against the wheel and was leaning forward just as the beer truck drew alongside and began to pass.

He thought at first, when he felt the impact against the left door, that he had allowed the Corvette to drift over and bump the truck's wheel. But then he saw, to his horror and amazement, that the Stingray had acquired an appendage, a streaky-faced, grimacing, orange-suited kid on a bicycle, gripping the rear-view mirror on the door and saying to Jeff through clenched teeth, "This . . . is . . . my . . . car!"

In his shock, Jeff allowed the car to swerve dangerously, and when he regained control, he aimed across the road toward a large parked truck. He wanted only to get rid of this parasitical kid, even if he had to squash him like a bug.

On the outside of the Stingray, Dantley saw the angular steel corners of the truck looming toward him very rapidly. Obviously, if he hung on he would die. He let go, braked, swung behind the Stingray as it accelerated, and looked back desperately for another ride. He spotted a brown Ford pickup about half a mile back; he pulled over to the right side of the road, began pumping, and shifted to eighth, to ninth, to tenth. He was grinning ferociously.

In the Corvette, meanwhile, Jeff was badly rattled. Not only had he briefly lost control of the car, but in the melee with Dantley he had dropped the lighted cigarette and could now smell it burning a hole in the carpet. He searched desperately but couldn't find it, and this threat, on top of the other perils that he had encountered in the last half hour, was the last straw. He lost his head, accelerated to a speed that was far from safe, even on a little-used service road, and headed straight for home. Later, he would regret this; he would wish fervently that he had driven far out into the desert, losing Dantley completely, and then returned by a roundabout route at his leisure.

He roared into the parking lot at Silverado, screeched to a skidding, dusty stop, ran to the bucket of windshield wash water at the pumps, and raced back with it to find and extinguish the smoldering cigarette. By the time Wayne reached him, drawn out of his office by all the commotion, Jeff had lost his cool entirely. He was almost inarticulate, capable only of monosyllables like "kid . . . bike . . ." and of flinging his arms and legs in a crazy pantomime of the chase. Even then, had he been a little more alert and less rattled, he would have escaped simply by driving the car around to the rear of the shop instead of leaving it out front, because the brilliant blob of color caught Dantley's eye the minute he rounded the curb toward Silverado, clinging to the box of the brown Ford pickup. Unfortunately, the pickup was going much faster than any of Dantley's other hosts, so that when he detached himself and pointed in the general direction of the Stingray, he shot with terrible speed across Silverado's front yard, past Wayne, Jeff, and the Corvette (screaming imprecations as he went), through the front doors, through the (fortunately empty) shop, and out the back. The last thing Kenny remembered about the whole furious chase was a large pile of old tires coming at him fast.

The first thing he remembered about the brief nightmare which followed was gradually becoming conscious of Wayne's face above his own and very close, so close that he could smell very expensive shaving lotion. "Hi, kid," Wayne was saying. "Remember me? Hm?" He was slapping Dantley's cheek, hard enough to sting. "I'm the guy who told you not to get mixed up with car thieves. Remember that? Remember me telling you you might get hurt? Hm?" he stood up. "Pick him up," he said. And when Jeff and Tony had lifted under his armpits and pulled the sagging Dantley to his feet, Wayne moved back half a step and swung all his weight into a vicious punch into Dantley's stomach which doubled him up, retching and gasping. Then he brought his clenched hands down on the back of Dantley's neck.

"Jesus," Jeff said, shaking violently. "You might have killed the guy!"

Wayne seized his shirt. "I might have to yet," he said. "And if I do it'll be because *you* were a damn fool. Remember that. Lock him up in the storeroom until I figure out what the hell we're gonna do. And put that car behind the shop."

What Wayne decided to do, finally, was to call Ed McGrath. McGrath groaned when he heard the news; he said that he'd cancel his summer-school classes for the rest of the week and get out to Vegas right away.

Later, Dantley began to revive. He hurt all over, and the first sign that he had that he was alive was pain— PAIN, and the fact that he could distinguish at least three levels of pain. First, there was the deep, dull ache which, as far as he could tell, he had from head to toe, radiating from every joint in his body. Second was the localized ache, intermittently dull and sharp like the pain in his stomach or the one in the back of his neck. Finally, there were several sharp, insistent pains, like

121

the one right between his eyes, or the ones from cuts on his hands where he had been slashed by various automotive appendages.

But, he decided, there was no doubt about it: he was alive, and if consciousness was an encouraging sign, he might stay alive for a little time yet. He opened his eyes. This action radically altered the levels of pain, making many sharp that had been dull. It hurt badly. He closed his eyes, then opened them again and kept them open.

At first he thought that he was in a cell, because the only light came from a single small window set high in the wall. But then, little by little as he ventured to move his eyeballs, he realized that he was in a storeroom, surrounded by an assortment of paint cans, spraying equipment, and tools. Slowly, groaning, he rose to his knees, then to his feet. He tried the door. Locked, of course. "Forget it, kid," said a voice from outside. "You're better off where you are."

Gently he sat down on an oil drum. The pain was ebbing slowly and his head was clearing. Around him, in the light that streamed in through the window high out of reach, he saw other drums of various sizes, some with tops, some without, and gradually the vision came to him of a nest of boxes that he had had as a child, one of his favorite toys because of its versatility; they could be fitted together, strung out along the floor, or—he remembered, beginning to smile, how they could be arranged to rise toward heaven, largest to smallest—stacked one on top of the other. Quietly he began to inspect the cans, discovering, in the process, a fifty-gallon one, half full of crankcase drippings. He began to evolve a plan.

Outside, Tony was applying the last strands of golden trim which would transform, finally, the Riviera that Monk had delivered two days before into a custom job of considerable interest and beauty. They had worked hard on it, and it would be ready for delivery tomorrow. Tony was not too bright; in fact his mind, like his body, was rather thick, but he possessed a doglike patience and great skill with the trim brush. He was also, in this one area, a perfectionist—an artist. Wayne had called him that once, clapping him on the back, and the word had pleased Tony so greatly that he had not bothered to ask for a raise after all. He worked patiently now, tracing golden filaments on the Riviera's gleaming flanks. He was alone. The radio purred sweet music.

Suddenly, from the storeroom where the kid was, there came a tremendous crash which startled Tony and caused him to deposit an ugly blob where there should have been a delicate curlicue. "What the hell's going on in there?" he shouted.

No answer.

Cursing, he got up and went to the door. "Hey," he said. "Kid. Don't cause no trouble, ya hear what I'm tellin ya? Just lay down and go to sleep or somethin'." He waited. "Hear me, kid?"

No answer.

Cursing more vehemently now, thinking of the ugly, fast-drying mark on the fender, Tony took the key from his pocket and opened the door. A breath of cool air hit him, drifting in through the open window. Scattered throughout the room were the collapsed remains of Dantley's ladder—drums, containers, cans.

"Holy shit!" Tony said. He spun around and rushed out of the room, snatching a length of chain from the workbench as he passed.

No sooner had the door slammed shut than Dantley appeared. He had not gone through the window but had hidden in the drum of crankcase oil and now emerged from it like a gasping, oil-drenched jack-in-the-box, to make a sloppy, sliding dash for the door and freedom. He paused only long enough on the way to wiggle a greasy finger down the length of Tony's careful paint job, destroying it completely, then he was through the door and away, oil spurting from his sneakers at every step.

Behind the shop, Tony quickly discovered that he had been tricked; there were no footprints in the dirt beneath the window, and there was no place for the kid to hide. He ran back inside, saw the mess in the storeroom, saw the slimy footprints leading through the front door and away, and saw—with a howl of rage—the greasy finger line irreparably smearing his paint. He burst through the front door hard in pursuit, the chain dangling menacingly from his wrist.

Probably he would have caught Kenny even if the boy had not had trouble in staying on his oil-smeared feet, for he was exhausted still from the bicycle adventure, and he hurt badly in many places, mainly his stomach. The harder he ran the more he hurt; he had to make frequent stops, doubled over and gasping for breath.

In one of these stops Tony caught up with him, and Tony's chain slashed down across his shoulders and felled him even before he knew the man was there. He writhed where he fell, partly from the ferocious new pain across his back, partly in a futile attempt to squirm away from another blow. Again the chain rose and fell, and Dantley cried out, half curse, half pleading. Again Tony's arm swung back, but this time, before he could strike he was caught in a glare of approaching headlights. Nor was it one car; it was several, all rumbling deeply and fanning out as they approached. Slowly, relentlessly, ominously they spread to cut off his path of escape. Tony wavered, cursing, then dropped the chain and bolted, held in the headlights until he swerved and darted up an alley a block and a half away.

Dantley could not have run even if he had been frightened, and he was too tired and too full of pain to be frightened anymore. He lay with one cheek on the cool pavement, and he watched the headlights come closer and closer, until he thought that they might actually be going to run over him. Then they stopped. Above the idling of the engines he heard sounds that he recognized from what seemed a long time ago—a click of a released latch, a whining of an electrical motor, a burst of mariachi music, and the tap of a gull-wing door touching the pavement. "Hey, there," said Tico, kneeling beside him. "Who the hell do you think you are, the last of the great oil sheiks?"

Dantley had trouble speaking. His lips felt like potatoes. "Hey, Tico," he said at last. "How about a lift?"

Others joined them. Dantley felt himself being picked up very gently and carried toward Tico's car. He hadn't meant that word *lift* literally, but he didn't protest.

Half an hour later, Vanessa was puzzled by a discreet tapping on the side door of the van. Harsh experience had taught her to check before opening the door in the night, and when she peered through the curtains she saw a grinning Mexican with all his pockets turned out and his hands palms-out toward her. "I'm clean," he was saying. "Just bringing home a friend." And, sure enough, two other Mexicans behind him were half carrying, half dragging Dantley toward her van. She gasped, and ran to open the door.

"Excuse us for bothering you, ma'am," Tico said, "but Kenneth has had a difficult day with honky friends, and our feeling is that he could use a warm shower and a bed for about ten hours. You agree?"

She could only nod dumbly, knuckles to her mouth. She almost did not recognize Kenny, he was so swollen and hunched, and after they had gone, with extravagant bowings and tippings of their hats, she drove him to the car wash around the corner. There, in the privacy of midnight, he stripped off all his clothes and stood submissively while Vanessa deposited a quarter and, with the dial set to WARM SUDS, sprayed him.

"Turn around," she said. "More."

He obliged, and she swept the fine, tingling spray up and down his body, washing away the grease and grime until he began to flinch from the spray on open sores.

And then, seeing them for the first time, she came to him and touched them with gentle fingers—the welts across his shoulders, and the coarse red mark on the back of his neck, the huge, spreading bruise above his belly button, and the various cuts and abrasions on his hands and arms. "Oh, Kenny!" she whispered. "Kenny!"

He submitted to her. He allowed her to wash him, and to dry him with a huge, soft towel that she had found somewhere in the van. And when he began to sag, he allowed her to slip one arm across her shoulders and to carry him, wrapped in the towel still, across the few yards of asphalt and into the comfort of the van and the ultimate comfort of her vast waterbed.

"Jeez," she said, caressing him, "they really knocked the shit out of you, didn't they?" He was too tired to open his eyes and see her, but she was weeping.

"Doesn't matter," he said. "Found it."

"You *found* it? You found the car?"

He nodded. "Know where it is."

"Oh, Kenny," she said, "I knew you would. I *knew* it!"

He went to sleep in her arms, and he dreamed marvelous dreams in which he stopped running and turned to confront his tormentors, and they dwindled into air and nothingness. Once, in the night, he awoke laughing.

Chapter Thirteen

———◆———

When Dantley awoke the next morning, Vanessa had already gone to work. She had left a note on her pillow: *DO IT!*

He got up very slowly, stiff and groaning. He found some milk and donuts in the refrigerator, and when he had eaten these, he drove downtown, feeling as if all the muscles in his body had been twisted like a wet towel. He parked. Slowly and with great difficulty he walked the half-block to the Las Vegas police station and began to climb the marble steps. He was halfway up when he heard someone call his name. "Hey, Kenny."

Incredulous, he turned, and there, ambling toward him, wearing a crooked, earnest smile of greeting, was McGrath.

"Hey!" Dantley said. "Far out!" Forgetting the pains in his back and shoulders, he hurried down the steps and seized his old teacher in an affectionate embrace. For a moment they shouted unintelligible greetings at each other, slapping and punching each other's shoulders.

"So. How are you?" McGrath asked.

"Fine! Terrific!"

"Yeah? Looks to me as if somebody worked you over a little bit."

"Ah, that's nothin'. The important thing is I found the car!" He laughed and hit McGrath's shoulder again. "How about that!"

"Great. Great news," McGrath said, but there was

pain in his smile and his eye was twitching, and he was looking down the street, not at Dantley. "I knew you would. Knew it all the time. Listen, let's go for a little drive, okay?"

"Yeah, well, the thing is, Mr. McGrath, I should get in there and report this. See, nobody knows about this but me. I mean, nobody knows where the car *is*, actually."

McGrath's hold on his shoulders was surprisingly firm. "No, no, no," he was saying, his eyes shut and his lips pursed. "It can wait. Not *that* much of a hurry." And then he was leading Dantley across the street to the familiar Dodge Maxi van that he had last seen surrounded by Kootz and Ricci and Kuchinsky and the others on the night the Stingray was stolen.

"Look, Mr. McGrath, why don't I go tell the cops and *then* we can go for a ride. Hey! That's it! You can come out when we go to pick it up. I'll show you where it is, and we'll get it back together. Neat, eh?"

"No, Kenny." McGrath looked as if he had a bad pain in his stomach which would never, ever, go away again. He sighed heavily. "The thing is, I *know* where the car is."

"You do?"

"Yeah. I do. Hop in and I'll tell you about it, okay?"

Gaping, Dantley climbed into the passenger's seat, and McGrath started the van and pulled out into the traffic, heading toward the airport. "You mean you've been doing your own detective work all this time?"

"Not quite." McGrath laughed harshly. "No, I wouldn't call it detective work."

"Well then, how do you . . . Ah, you don't know. You're putting me on!"

"Silverado Auto Body," McGrath said, driving. "And Paint. Special Cars for Special People, right?"

Dantley nodded slowly. "Yeah," he whispered. "Right."

"Even know the boss: Wayne Lowry. Right?"

Dantley nodded. "How . . ."

"Because he was a student of mine. Class of 'sixty-two. The best student I ever had until you came along."

Dantley frowned, looking hard at McGrath. The older man was driving doggedly, his face working. "Look, kid, what I've got to tell you is something about life. okay? It's not easy, but I figure that, well, that's a teacher's job, isn't it? To teach? To show young people what life is about? Isn't that true? So okay. The fact is that Wayne and me, well, we're kinda like partners, you know what I mean?"

Dantley's face looked very long and pale under the peaked cap. He had begun to shiver, although he was sitting in the sun. "You mean you're *in* this? You mean you stole the *Stingray?*"

"Kenny. Kenny. Listen. You gotta understand this. You gotta see how it is. There's more to it than just that. That's not fair, you know what I mean? You can't over*simplify*, Kenny. Jeez, you know, that's one of the things wrong with the world today—people want to make life too simple. They want to explain things away, you know what I mean? When really, life is very complicated, very complex, and a lot of it can't be explained. Take motives, for instance."

"Motives," said Dantley.

"Yeah. Like, why people *really* do the things they do." McGrath had begun to perspire lightly. They were in the suburbs, now. Heat hazes shimmered and washed across the road in front of them. "God knows it's not exactly my field, but you can't live on this earth for forty-three years, like I have, and not see that sometimes you can be forced to do bad things for good reasons. You understand that?"

"No," Dantley said.

"Well. take me, for example, okay? I'm a little guy . . . jeez, you know what I make a year? Fifteen grand That's all. A lousy fifteen grand. And every year for the past few years it's been about the same—

thirteen, fourteen, fifteen. So alright, you can say that I'm doing the same job, right? Fair enough, but I'm living in the same house, and the cost of that's gone up more than a thousand a year—water, taxes, repairs, and all the rest of it. And food. And insurance. And trying to put something by for the kids' education, and a little bit to take the wife away for two weeks once a year. Well, the thing is, I can't do it! I'm caught, Kenny! I'm just a little guy, and I'm caught! Either I gotta sacrifice—and that means hurting the wife and kids—or else I gotta find something else. So I find something else; I teach night school. Still not enough. I teach summer school. *Still* not enough. What am I gonna do, Kenny? You tell me. Here I am, I try to do my level best, I try to do a good job. But I'm getting *old*, Kenny. And I'm fallin' farther and farther behind every year. *Nothin' I do is enough!* Have you ever . . . Naw, you don't even know what that means, do you?"

"Sure I do," Dantley said. "It's what happens when you take English, and math, and history."

McGrath laughed bitterly. "Yeah. Well, maybe you *do* know. Anyway, one night I get a phone call. Friend of mine. Another teacher. And he makes me a proposition that gives me a way out. I mean, *really* a way out. Okay, so it's illegal, but nobody really gets hurt except the insurance companies, and they can afford it, right?"

"Nobody gets hurt," Dantley echoed.

"Right. Nobody. But what I began to tell you, what it's really important for you to see is that I didn't do it for myself, I did it for other people. See? You can end up doing something that's wrong *for good reasons*." McGrath tried to laugh. He attempted to convey to Dantley a full appreciation of absurdity in that laugh; but he failed. It emerged a small and pathetic thing, a mere whine of incredulity.

"Oh, Jesus," Dantley said. "Jesus." He was sitting with his hands pressed between his knees, and he was shivering violently.

They had reached the airport bypass. McGrath

pulled off onto the shoulder and stopped. A 727 lumbered overhead, leaving dust behind, and a settling stench of burned fuel oil, and a vast emptiness. Around them lay the stripped and burned-out carcasses of abandoned automobiles.

"Who was the other teacher?" Dantley's voice was thin and tiny, like an insect's. "Who stole the car?"

"Forrie," McGrath said, sighing. "Forrie Redman. Hooked up his Blazer, towed it away."

"I shoulda known," Dantley said. "I never did trust that sonuvabitch."

"Look, kid." McGrath had shifted around to face Dantley, one arm resting on the back of the seat, the other on the steering wheel, his hands making small, aimless gestures as he talked. "I'm a teacher, right? Maybe I'm not a very good one. Maybe I'm not very honest, and maybe I'm not very bright. I don't know. But what I do know is that a teacher has to teach what he's learned himself."

"You already said that."

"Yeah. But what I want to tell you now is that guys like you and me, guys that work with their hands, well, we can get somehow caught. I don't know how it happens; maybe it's different for everyone. But all I know is that we're caught. We're behind. And we never catch up, no matter how hard we try. That's the God's truth, Kenny. You can learn it the hard way or you can learn it the easy way. I'd say you're a lucky man to learn it young enough so that you make the right moves, keep ahead."

Dantley was sitting as in a trance, his eyes fixed unmoving at some point on McGrath's dashboard. He had stopped shivering.

"And," McGrath went on, opening his hands, "when I say 'keep ahead' I'm talking about seven hundred dollars a week. Take home. Think about that for a minute. Seven hundred, Kenny."

Dantley stared.

"We sell to rich people. You can cook up the wildest

131

custom cars you ever dreamed of, *and you can make 'em*, not just draw pretty pictures on a scrap of paper. Why, Kenny, this might be the best thing that ever happened to you, talent like yours."

"How come you never said anything? We laid up all that fiberglass and you never said a thing."

"How was I to know you'd fall in love with the car? I didn't know that. Anyway, I tried to tell you. Remember, I tried to tell you? Kenny, I said, don't get too attached to that thing. Remember, it's only a hunk of metal, after all. It's only a *thing*, a commodity. Remember that?"

Dantley nodded slowly. "You were lying, weren't you. Mr. McGrath. You knew you were gonna steal it. You knew it was more than just another car. You said once it was a work of art, remember?"

"Yeah," McGrath said.

"Hours and hours and hours we spent on it. You even said once that that's one of the things that makes a work of art: time. Concentrated time, you said."

"Okay. Sure. I said that." McGrath nodded heavily.

"You know what I wanted to do? Hell, I never wanted to own the car. I knew I couldn't do that. I knew I'd *never* have enough money for that. But I just wanted to drive it up and take my mother for a little ride. I was gonna ask you. I don't know why, it was just something I wanted to do." He laughed. "You know, maybe if I'd *done* that and then you'd stolen it, I wouldn't have minded so much."

For a few minutes neither of them spoke. Then McGrath said, "As a matter of fact, I saw your mother."

"Yeah?"

He nodded. "I drove out to see her. I nearly missed her. She was moving."

"Moving?"

McGrath nodded. "To Del Mar. They were just packing up when I got there." He saw Dantley looking at him and shrugged. "There was a man. LTD."

"Oh, yeah. Mr. Borodino."

"Anyway, your mom said she figured you'd find her if you wanted to, down in Del Mar, and she asked me to give you these." He reached behind him and passed Dantley a large brown envelope. Outside was printed one word, *Kenny*. The boy opened it and there slid into his lap all the photographs and clippings that had once ringed his bedroom. A few fluttered to the floor; among them were the photographs of the laughing, crew-cut young man lounging against the fender of his machine. There was no note: only the pictures.

"Home isn't where it used to be," McGrath said.

Dantley was gathering up the pictures one by one and tucking them back into the envelope. He said nothing.

"Come on in with us, kid. Please."

"It's okay, Mr. McGrath. I won't tell the cops. I won't tell anybody."

McGrath shook his head. "We can't take that chance, kid. At least Wayne can't. Take a look behind."

Dantley twisted around. Parked at the rear was his beloved Stingray, and lounging behind the wheel, with an expensive pair of tooled cowboy boots sticking out of the passenger's window, was Wayne. He was wearing sunglasses, and he was smiling.

"He says," McGrath went on, "That either you're in or you're out. And if I don't flick my taillights in another"—he checked his watch—"minute, he's gonna come over and handle it his way. I'm sorry, kid. There's nothing I can do. I'm caught, see. I'm caught."

Dantley looked away from him, out past the highway, past the low, squalid scattering of anonymous workshops and repairshops, past the airport where the big jets had been landing and taking off throughout their conversation, past the desert itself to the beckoning line of purple hills in the distance.

"Okay, sir," he said after a minute. "I'll do whatever you say. I'll do whatever you think is best."

"This is best, kid. Believe me," McGrath said, and he pressed his brake pedal three times, very slowly.

Later that night, Vanessa returned from work to find Dantley lying on the waterbed, hands behind his head, in the dark. "Hey," she said, sliding the door closed behind her, "what's the matter? Why're you in the dark?" She switched the light on.

He rolled over on his stomach and buried his face in the pillow.

"I brought us some food," she said. "See?" There were hamburgers, and cans of Coke with straws sticking up like bunny ears, and bowls of french fries with thick gravy.

"Turn the light off, please."

She did that, setting the tray down. "What is it, Kenny?"

"Nothing."

"Did you go to the police?"

"Yes," he said. "No." His voice was muffled in the pillow.

"What? What do you mean? Did you get the car?"

"No, I didn't get the car."

"You didn't . . . Well, what . . . ?"

"Look," Dantley said, lifting his face out of the pillow, but not speaking toward her, speaking instead straight down toward the pillow, "I just don't want to talk about it, okay? Can we just forget it?"

"Okay," she said. "All right. Want to go for a walk?" She waited. "It's real nice out. There are stars."

"No," he said.

She stood looking at him for a minute, and then she picked up a hamburger and a plate of french fries, took them up into the front of the van where a bit of light was shining through the windshield, and she began to eat.

Chapter Fourteen

"It's nine-thirty," Wayne said.

"He's coming, he's coming," McGrath said. "He promised. He'll be here."

They were sitting in the office at Silverado. Sunlight filtered dimly through the filthy windows and spilled across the desk—on the litter of paper, pens and spare parts, on the two half-empty coffee cups, on Wayne's cowboy boots.

"Why didn't you pick him up?" Wayne asked. "Just to be sure."

"Because he wouldn't let me. I offered but he said no, he'd do it himself. I tell you, that's just the kind of kid he is—a loner, you know? But he'll be here. He will be. Relax."

McGrath himself, however, looked anything but relaxed. His frown was deeper than ever, he was chewing at the cuticle of a forefinger, and he was standing, peering through the window and up the road toward Las Vegas. He was tremendously relieved when a car pulled off onto the shoulder and Dantley stepped out and slammed the door, giving the driver a two-fingered wave of thanks as he did so. The boy striding across the gravel toward the shop, however, was a very different person from the one McGrath had dropped off at the parking lot the day before. That Dantley looked, talked, and walked as if he had been given another physical beating; this one approached with his head up, and his shoulders back, and—McGrath could see, just under the shadow of the low-set hat brim—a kind of tough smile. *Determined*, McGrath thought first; then he thought, *caught!*, and he knew then what was familiar about the walk of the boy—it was the way he himself used to go into work when he had believed that it was only for a little while, and that there was a way out the other end. "Here he is," he said.

They went out into the shop to meet him. "First thing," Wayne said, shaking hands, "I wanna tell you I'm sorry for the other day."

Dantley shrugged.

"I guess you might say I overreacted a little." He laughed.

"You might say that," Dantley said.

"Me too." Tony came over, wiping his hands on a rag. "About that chain. Sorry."

"Yeah, well"—Dantley took his hand—"sorry about messing up your pinstriping. That was nasty. Real nasty."

"And Jeff." Wayne said, "you've already met."

Grinning, Jeff shook hands. "All I can say is, you ride one hell of a bicycle!"

"About that bicycle," Wayne said. "It's hot, right? I've been thinking, maybe we ought to do a paint job and resell it. Let Monk run it out to San Diego." They all laughed except Dantley.

"Pay," Dantley said. "Seven hundred a week's not enough. I start at eight-fifty."

There was a moment of shocked silence, and then Jeff said, "Eight-fifty! Holy shit, that's more than twice . . ."

"First week in advance," Dantley said.

Wayne silenced Jeff with a hand on his arm. He was looking hard at Dantley, and he was smiling a very thin smile. "Kid," he said, "That's just the way I'd play it myself. We got a bargain, and I should know, because I've been driving around the Corvette, right?"

"Yeah." Dantley said. "Right. Exactly. And that's another part of the deal: sometimes I get to drive it."

"Okay." Wayne laughed. "Fair enough. Now let's go

136

to work. When the others had returned to their jobs, Wayne took Dantley into his office and counted eight hundred and fifty dollars out of the desk drawer. "You did say in advance, didn't you?"

"Thanks," Dantley said, pocketing the cash.

"Now, then." Wayne was smiling. He came around the desk and put an arm across Dantley's shoulders. "Let me show you the first little job I'd like you to do." They went out to the rear of the shop, where the Corvette rested in splendor. "Right across here," Wayne said, indicating the top of the driver's door, "I want you to paint *Wayne's Wheels*. Classy, eh? I'll leave the style and all that up to you, but I want it in black, gold-trimmed. Okay?"

"Yes, sir. Just fine." Dantley said.

"See you later, then." And smiling to himself, Wayne returned inside the shop.

Carefully, slowly, using all his skill and craft, over the following two hours Dantley did the job that had been requested of him, and when it was nearly finished, the others began to gather and peer admiringly over his shoulder. Even Tony was there, nodding his compliments.

When he had finished, Dantley cleaned up briskly and went inside to be given another job, and then another, and another, all of which he completed quickly and perfectly. In mid-afternoon he helped to unload two cars off the purple-blue Kenworth trailer, fascinated by the antics of the Monk. When McGrath left for the drive back to Los Angeles, just before quitting time, Dantley said goodbye to him and shook hands in a way that chilled McGrath to the very bone, so empty was it of any feeling whatsoever. Dantley's eyes looked at him; Dantley's voice spoke to him and wished him a safe drive, but clearly Dantley's respect and affection had gone. McGrath earnestly wanted to take the boy by the shoulders and explain, *explain*. But he did not know what he could have said to make any difference.

137

Anyway, before he had a chance to say anything, Dantley had turned away and gone back to work.

That evening, Vanessa was emptying trash into one of the receptacles when she was startled by a sharp pat on her bottom. "Hey!" she said, spinning around with the wastebasket half raised. Then she caught her breath and pressed a knuckle against her lip. Dantley stood before her transformed. His lanky hair had been cut and deftly styled. His threadbare cap had vanished, as, indeed, had all his old clothes, to be replaced by a resplendent costume—frilled, high-collared shirt, velvet sport jacket, generously flared trousers, and elaborately tooled cowboy boots.

"I know the name," Vanessa said when she regained control, "I just can't think of the face." And there was something about the face that frightened her, something that went with the clothes.

"Come on," he said, taking her arm. "We're going out." And he led her, protesting, back to the van and, giving her only ten minutes to free her hair of its curlers and to brush it out as they went, drove straight to the parking lot of the hotel.

"I thought you didn't like this place," she said.

"That was yesterday. I couldn't afford it then."

"Kenny, I can't go in there!"

"Sure you can." Again he had taken her arm and was leading her toward the door.

"I can't! Look at me! They won't let me!"

"Sure they will."

And they did. The next few hours, Vanessa decided later, were probably the most exciting and bewildering of her life. She was taken first to the dress shop where Dantley selected and bought her the kind of gown she always longed to own. She gasped when she saw the price tag, and whispering, she tried unsuccessfully to protest to Dantley. He hurried her on—to buy shoes, to buy jewelry, to buy makeup, all of which he paid for from a squeaky-new pigskin wallet. "Kenny, what's happened? Are you crazy? Did you rob a *bank* or something? For godsake *tell* me!" But he told her nothing, not even when they were alone in the hotel room. When she came out of the shower there was champagne in a silver pail with a little white towel draped over the bottle, and they sipped this while she dressed and touched up her face. And then they went down to the casino, where Kenny tipped waitresses lavishly for complimentary cocktails, and gambled on a large scale and, incredibly, won.

Later, when they were in the canopied bed in the huge hotel room, he said, "This is the way to go, isn't it? From now on this is the way it's going to be. Real living. No more sleeping in vans and trucks and no more eating french fries and crap like that."

"Kenny, I think I know what you've done. You found your car, and you got it back, and you *sold* it, didn't you?"

"Naw . . ." He laughed harshly.

"Well *tell* me, *tell* me!" She beat his chest with her fist. "Where did you get all this *money?*"

"Made it. Earned it. Got a job."

"Where. What kind of job?"

"Body shop. We do custom work. Special cars for special people. Thing is, they pay eight-fifty a week, first week in advance. Real nice fellas."

"Eight-fifty?"

"To start. I expect to go up from there."

She pulled away from him and sat up. "But what about your car? Aren't you . . . aren't we going to look for it anymore?"

He shook his head. "Naw. Look, that really is kid stuff. I've grown up a little, last couple of days."

"You mean you're going to let them get *away* with it?"

Again he laughed, a harsh laugh that frightened her. "Look, what's a car? A car is just a commodity to be bought and sold, right? Like anything. A piece of tin. As a matter of fact, you knew it all along, didn't you? You always wanted to be a hooker, right? And that's

139

what I figured out, the last couple of days: *anything* can be bought if you got the money. And it's all right. It's *all right*, see?"

She had been watching him unblinkingly as he spoke. "I know what happened," she said. "You did find it, didn't you? You found it and they bought you off. You're working for *them*, aren't you, Kenny?" She sat up suddenly as the realization hit her.

He smiled and spread his hands. "What's it matter *who* you work for, as long as the pay's good?"

"What's it *matter*? Are you kidding?" She swung out of bed and stood naked confronting him, crouched, her face a blend of shock and increasing rage. Her hands came away from her mouth and began to clench into fists.

He could not meet her gaze. "Look, look, look," he was saying, "just take it easy. Did you hear what I told you? Eight-fifty a week! That's a lotta money, kiddo."

"Horse shit!"

"It's a lot of money!"

"It's peanuts! It's nothing! If *I* wanted to sell out, I could make that overnight!"

"Whadya mean, sell out? I just took a job, that's all. What are you . . ."

"It's not just a job! It's not!" She began to flail at him, her small fists battering indiscriminately on his chest, his arms, his head. "You dummy! You klutz! Don't you see what you're doing?"

He managed to seize and hold her wrists. "Listen, the car, it doesn't matter. Really."

"*I* know that," she said. "It's *you* that matters!"

But he went on, disregarding her. "Pretty soon, with this kinda money, I can have any car I want—Corvette, Cadillac, Lamborghini . . ."

"Lamborghini," she said, collapsing, and the word was like a long, soft wail. "Oh, Kenny!"

"Yeah. And nobody gets hurt, that's the beautiful thing."

"Nobody gets hurt," she said.

140

"Everybody wins. You too."

Very slowly, she sank back away from him. She began to shudder, crouched on the bed, and she drew a blanket around her shoulders. "He doesn't even *see*," she said, spreading her hands, as if appealing to some third person.

"As a matter of fact, I figure it's time you started to win too. I figure I should be a paying customer just the way you wanted me to be that first time, remember?" He found a hundred-dollar bill in his wallet and withdrew it. "After all, why should you put out for nothing? You oughta ask for what you're worth."

For a long minute they looked at each other with the bill between them. Then, very slowly, her head sank forward until it rested on his chest. "Kenny," she said. "Kenny, I don't want that."

"Well, I'm gonna give it to you anyway." He reached over and dropped it on her pillow.

She did not move, and when he brushed the hair back from her face, his fingers came away wet with tears.

Chapter Fifteen

———◆———

The following morning he took a taxi to work.

"Hey," Wayne said, greeting him, "you better start thinking about your own set of wheels, man."

"Keep an eye out for me," Dantley said, passing him. "Something with a little class." In the storeroom he climbed into his overalls. He was terribly unhappy, and angry at his unhappiness. After all, he had, he told himself, no real reason for this disgruntlement; he was surrounded by cars, he was doing exactly what he used to love to do, and he was being extremely well paid. Why was it, then, that he felt poorer than he had ever been—even when he was living in a U-Haul trailer with a furniture pad for a blanket?

"Supervise today," Wayne said, sticking his head into the storeroom. "Give the other boys a few pointers."

Dantley nodded acknowledgement. He supervised most of the morning—helping Tony cut open the body of a Plymouth Fury for rebuilding, helping Jeff set the correct scoop position on a freshly puttied 442. They accepted his suggestions because they made obvious sense; it was clear from the outset that he was far ahead of them in both practical knowledge and design theory. He gave his instructions quietly and clearly, and when both men were working adequately on their own, he retired to a third work bay, where the gleaming black Trans Am awaited his attentions. On the wall was a large profile drawing of the car, with red lines indicating modifications. He began to work on the front end, taking measurements, taking notes, and he was still working on this job later in the morning when, to his astonishment, and delight, Vanessa's van slid past the window. Smiling, he laid down his tools and went outside, and he was just rounding the rear of the van when the driver stepped out.

The driver was very fat. He was wearing a pair of khaki trousers which had lost a battle with his stomach and retreated far below his naval. His dirty Hawaiian sport shirt bulged in little oval openings between buttons, revealing his hairy front. Pulled low over his eyes was a yellow cap with a "Caterpillar" flash above the brim. His jowls were stubbled; unlaced running shoes flopped on his bare feet. "Hey," he was calling to Wayne, "I want you guys should paint out this here name, Vanessa. I want it should say instead, across there, PETE'S PULSATOR."

Wayne had just begun to explain that Silverado never touched vans, and that the driver ought to try Orlando's down the street, when Dantley moved. He had been so shocked by the appearance of this person when he had expected Vanessa, that he had stood for stunned moments at the rear of the van; but then something clicked—he actually *heard* a click—inside his head, and all the suppressed rage, and frustration, and shame, and disappointment that had been building in him over the previous two days gushed out. He was on the man before he even realized what he was doing—seizing his fatty shoulders and spinning him so that they were eye-to-eye. "What the fu . . ." the man began.

"Where is she?" Dantley snarled.

"Who? Who the hell you talking about? Take your goddamn hands off me! You *crazy?*"

"You stole this van."

"I didn't steal it; I just bought it."

"Bullshit! You're a goddamn car thief!"

"Listen, Mac. You take a look at that windshield and I'll give you all the bullshit you can eat!"

143

Warily, Dantley let go and moved around to the front. CHERRY, the sign on the windshield said, $2500.

"Okay, okay," the fat man was saying. "So what'd'ya want now, smart-ass? Ya wanna see my receipt? Ya wanna see my ownership papers?"

"Sorry," Dantley said.

"I guess you should goddamn well be sorry!" He waggled a finger in Dantley's face. "You wanna be careful who ya go around callin' a car thief, because somebody might just take it outta your hide, kid."

Dantley spun. The adrenalin was still pumping through him, and what he suddenly saw was a thin curtain of red, descending like a veil of blood, between him and the fat driver. In a terrible silence, teeth bared, he lunged for the man's throat, as he had once gone for Kootz, as he had gone for Jeff, and had Wayne not interferred, he might have strangled him. But Wayne moved into his path smoothly and easily, blocking him and saying to the fat man at the same time, "Try Orlando's down the street. He's the man you want. He'll do that little job for you."

Reluctantly, the man climbed into his van and gripped the wheel with both hands, an action which for some reason sent Dantley into renewed paroxysms of fury. "You wanna watch what kinda maniacs you hire, fella. Guy like that's liable to get you sued!" And with much roaring of the engine, he drove away.

"You know," Wayne said, turning to Dantley when the van had gone, "the funniest thing about all of that was you calling that guy a car thief."

"Mistake," Dantley said.

"But you fail to see the humor?"

"Yeah, I fail. What's funny?"

"Because, my friend, what do you think *you* are?"

"I'm . . ." Dantley began, and then stopped when he realized that they were all laughing at him—Wayne, and Jeff and Tony too. "Okay," he said. "Joke. Look, I need a car. Just for an hour or two."

144

Wayne shrugged. "Your own time," he said.

"Sure."

"How's the Trans Am? Finished?"

"Nearly."

"Take it."

So Dantley took it. He took it back down the Strip, reveling despite his anxiety about Vanessa, in the brute power and stability of the machine, reveling in the rumble of its exhaust and the menacing hiss of the carbureator under its cowl. It was not the Corvette, of course, but he decided that it was a close second.

He tried first the drive-in restaurant where Vanessa had last worked, knowing before he asked for her through the ordering box that she would not be there, and not surprised at all by the growling proprietor who told him that she hadn't appeared for work that morning, and that, furthermore, she owed him for three meals.

Somewhere between the restaurant and the first hotel the enormity of what he had done the night before suddenly struck him. He realized, free now of the effects of too many drinks, and too much bravado, and too much brutal arrogance and shame, how he had betrayed her. For the first time he was able to see himself through Vanessa's eyes. What he saw was that his tireless quest for his car was simply something that she had never encountered before—an incidence of a man *not* selling out—and that it had kindled in her a kind of admiration and a kind of hope. When it was clear to her that he *had* sold out, she had simply decided to do the same thing, to take what she could get, and so she had sold first the van, and then . . .

Somewhere between the drive-in and the hotel, Kenny Dantley figured out, step by step, exactly what he would have to do.

She was nowhere to be found in the first hotel, or the second, or the third, and although he tipped the doormen lavishly, none of them could remember her arrival, although all three pretended to think hard. In the fourth, however, the Silver Bird, he found her. He strode through the casino, very out of place in his sweaty and paint-spattered T-shirt, and as he approached the baccarat table, a knot of people opened to reveal her, but he almost passed out without recognizing her.

She was transformed. She was wearing a low-cut black dress and a velvet choker. Her hair was swept up in a sophisticated chignon, and her eyes were made heavier and broader, darkened with mascara. The hand that rested on the edge of the table shimmered with long, lacquered nails.

She looked right through him, and he paused in his advance on her, uncertain for a moment that it really was she. Then he went on. "Hey," he said.

"Have we met?"

"What d'ya mean, have we met? Let's go." He took her arm, but an older man—perhaps thirty-eight, perhaps forty—heavy but well built and nattily dressed (*a Buick salesman on vacation*, Dantley thought) moved between them, saying, " 'Scuse me, fella," to Dantley and handing something to Vanessa. "Here you go, Rosalind, honey. Play with these."

"But I'm losing all your *chips*, Mr. Blanchard." She looked up at him through her lashes, and her voice a good imitation of Marilyn Monroe's.

"*Ros*alind . . ." Dantley began.

"Doesn't matter, baby. There's lots more where those came from. Now, how about a little drink. More of the same?"

"I could go for that," she said, and smiled. When he had headed off to the bar she put a hand on her hip, leaned on the table, and looked hard at Dantley. "Straight A's in dramatic arts. Never told you that, did I?"

"What is this Rosalind crap?"

"My new name. You like?"

"No, I don't like. Let's go."

"Sorry, I'm otherwise engaged."

146

"You . . . you *did* it. You're a *hooker!*"

She moved close to him, so close that he could smell the faint odor of gin on her breath. "That's right, Kenny," she whispered. "Just like you!"

"Whassis? Whassis?" Smiling, the Buick salesman worked his way between them again, bearing two drinks. "Here ya go, honey." He looked Dantley up and down. "Who's your friend?"

"My cousin Homer," she said. "He does body work, too."

"Body work! Terrific!" He clamped a hammy arm over Dantley's shoulders. "Listen, How'd'ya like to join the party a little later? Room 619. Few friends are droppin' in and one of em, I know for sure, would go for your kind of body work Homer, m'boy."

Dantley ignored him. "You coming?"

She shook her head.

The salesman laughed. "Where you expect her to go, fella? This little lady and I have an understanding, right, honey? A one-hundred-dollar understanding. Got it, Homer? And you are *way* back in the line." Winking, he led Vanessa away.

When they reached the elevator, still carrying their drinks, she looked back. Then they were gone.

Dantley turned and ran. He ran through the lobby, through the swinging door, past the doorman who said something unintelligible to him. He ran through the parking lot, dodging cars moving and parked, until he came to the Trans Am. Then he fell on the hood and pounded and pounded and pounded it until his rage had spent itself and his fist hurt so much he could pound no more.

"Whazzamatter?" asked a passerby. "Got a lemon?"

He drove back to Silverado. He drove tensely but not fast. He knew exactly what he had to do, and he knew how he would go about it.

For the rest of the afternoon he worked steadily, carefully. From time to time, glancing around him, he even whistled—"Something in the Way She Moves"—

desperately off-key. But he made sure that when closing time came and Wayne called to him, "Hey, enough. How about a beer," he was in the middle of a job that couldn't be left. "Okay," Wayne shrugged, departing. "Make sure the lights are out and the doors are locked when you leave, will you?"

He listened to the Trans Am head down the road and into the distance, Wayne winding it out into the straightaways; and when the sound had faded completely, when the only other sounds in the night were the buzzing of insects, and the humming of the neons above his head, and the occasional passing of indifferent cars, he switched off the lights in the adjacent showroom where the Corvette lay in sleek spendor, and he walked into the showroom and around the car, finding his way by the reflected light of the shop neons, brushing his hand across the car's flanks as he went. Then he switched off the shop lights as well, and opened the door that led from the showroom to the outside, and with ludicrous ease, despite the fact that Wayne had the keys, he made some connections behind the ignition of the Stingray, and started it and drove it out into the night. For an instant he was tempted simply to keep going—to put his foot on the gas and spray sand and dust all over Silverado Auto Body. But he resisted; he swung back. After he had opened the outside doors of the shop, he guided the car into the painting bay.

All night he worked. He began by sweeping his spraygun across the repugnant "Wayne's Wheels," back and forth until the words had vanished entirely beneath gleaming lacquer. Then he worked outward, over the doors over the fenders and the hood, over the roof and the trunk. Carefully, inch by inch he covered the entire car, and then, stripping off the newspaper and masking tape which had covered the glass and chrome, he moved it forward into the drying oven. After the first had dried, he began laboriously to give it a second coat.

Later that night, a lone coyote approached cautiously from the desert, sniffing the odor of paint that drifted downwind from Silverado, and skirting the dim rectangles of artificial light that sprawled from the windows. For a moment he listened to the pumping of the compressor and the whirr of fans inside, cocking first one ear and then the other, and then, deciding that there was nothing here to interest him, he loped off in the direction of Las Vegas and the succulent garbage available in dumps, cans, in piles of plastic bags behind the drive-ins, everywhere around the fabulous city.

The night wore on. From time to time, cars whizzed past Silverado in both directions, but no one paid any attention to the dim light shining at the back of the shop; it was, after all, a city that never slept.

Morning came in stages not of white but of red, the blood red first of the sun on low clouds, growing by the second more intense, more brilliant, until at last it vanished altogether. It gave way to the glow of the sun itself and to the high vermilion mares' tails sweeping away in all directions. It would be a hot day.

At eight, Tony and Jeff arrived at Silverado together. They got out of Tony's modified Camaro together, walked to the big bay door together, unlocked it, and together, swung it up. What confronted them caused them both to stop dead. Tony actually dropped his lunch pail.

Facing them was the Corvette; but not the Corvette they had left in the showcase on the previous evening. This was the Stingray as it had first come to them, rolling down the ramp from Monk's truck—candy-apple red with iridescent orange flames sweeping across its air dam and down its flanks. The engine was idling.

"What the . . ." Jeff stepped inside the door, and was felled almost instantly by a blow above the temple. Dantley stepped out of the shadows and across his prostrate form, moving toward Tony, rubber mallet poised. But the older man moved with surprising agility; before Dantley could stop him he had crossed to his workbench and seized, once again, a length of chain. He turned, smiling viciously, wrapping it around his hand as he did so. "Smart-ass kid," he said. "Think ya know everything, eh? Well, now I'm gonna teach ya not to order Tony around." And he moved in.

Dantley backed up, tripped, fell, squirmed desperately out of the way as the first blow lashed into the concrete beside his head, kicking chips of stone into the side of his face.

"And this time," Tony said, raising the chain with terrifying deliberation, "this time there won't be no goddamn chicanos to pick up the pieces."

Dantley watched the chain swing upward in a slow-motion arc like action in some dreams, dreams of terrible pursuit. He flung out his hands, desperately hoping to grasp something substantial by which he could pull himself out of the way, or with which he could defend himself, and what he felt, to his joy, was the handle of the spraygun, still loaded and charged to peak pressure. He aimed, squeezed. Blobs of red lacquer instantly filled Tony's nostrils and eye sockets, sending him reeling backward, stumbling and choking, falling into a clutter of equipment in the corner of the shop.

Dantley got into the waiting Stingray and closed the door. He was shaking, but he managed smoothly to put the car into gear and drive through the open doors of the bay. Outside, he swung toward the highway, kicking a splume of dust and gravel over and into Silverado Auto Body. By the time Jeff had revived and Tony had managed more or less to cleanse himself of lacquer, Dantley was a mile down the highway toward Las Vegas, and accelerating.

Chapter Sixteen

———◆———

Room 619, the Buick salesman had said, just before he led Vanessa away.

Dantley could not get that image out of his mind— the man with his arm around her, and Vanessa looking back at him just before she had stepped into the elevator. He knew that despite herself she had been making a plea to him—"Get me out of this! Save me!"—and the knowledge drove him on, grimly, even pushing to one side the delight he knew he should be feeling in driving the Corvette again.

Las Vegas was beginning to move with the life of a new day. The suburbs were waking up; sleepy-eyed fathers were driving to work; mothers were stepping out onto porches, holding their bathrobes closed while they stooped for the morning paper; and children, singly and in little groups, were trotting over cross-walks under the watchful eyes of yellow-gloved attendants. On the Strip itself, however, the real Las Vegas, morning made little difference. It was only another small stage in the care and maintenance of the city's major business. Shifts changed in the bars, the restaurants, the casinos. Daytime doormen appeared, looking relatively fresh, and night doormen went home, looking rumpled and weary as they walked to their cars in their motley and bizarre uniforms, like the stragglers of some nocturnal battle. The city slept; the city awoke. But the sound of the city's coursing lifeblood went on uninterrupted— the whisper of cards on green tables, the murmuring of croupiers and dealers, the clatter of spinning wheels, the rattling of slot machines.

At the Silver Bird, Dantley was the first event of the doorman's morning. He had just come on duty, was just stretching up on his toes and raising his face to the sun of this new day, when the Corvette swept around the curved entrance and rocked to a stop right in front of the door. Dantley jumped out and ran past him into the hotel, and by the time the doorman had reached the driver's side of the car and realized that there were no keys inside, it was too late to call him back. So the Corvette sat, resplendent and immovable, blocking the entire driveway. Already another car was coming up behind it; already a line was forming. Drivers were beginning to grow angry. Soon they would be honking. The doorman returned to the shadows beside the door. He rocked gently from his toes to his heels. He watched the rising sun through the patient eyes of a native American. He waited.

Inside, Dantley had crossed the lobby at a run, seen that the elevators were all engaged, and taken the stairs. By the time he reached the sixth floor he was badly winded, and had to pause, bent over and gasping, holding onto the railing. But when he found Room 619 he revived. He heard voices and laughter inside. He tried the door, discovered it was locked, stepped back, and kicked. The door burst open with a sound of splintering wood and brass screws hitting the parquet floor.

"What the . . . Who are you? What do you think . . ." The first person that Dantley met inside was a pudgy and unwholesome-looking fellow in his early fifties. His face was pockmarked; his lanky black hair hung down over his collar. He was in the act of pouring himself a drink when Dantley entered, and he had begun to swing the bottle of whiskey back, clearly intending to use it as a club, when Dantley reached him, lifted him clean off his feet with a blow to the jaw from the heels of both hands, and sent him crashing backward over a coffee table and the sofa. Another man was in the room, a small, rat-faced person who backed away, waving both hands in front of him, as Dantley approached. "Rosalind," he said. "You want Rosalind, right? She's in there, in there," and he pointed to the bathroom.

There were voices in the bathroom, and a sound of sloshing water, like that caused by someone getting up out of a full tub. And there were also very bright lights. When Dantley reached the door, these lights swung toward him, blinding him until he found the cord and yanked it out of its socket. Then, in the soft bathroom fluorescent, he saw that the lights were film floodlamps held by a red-haired woman in a pink jumpsuit, and that the sloshing sound he had heard was made by a middle-aged man in a skindiver's black wetsuit. He was standing in a tub of water; he was cradling a 16mm Bolex camera, and his brow was creased with alarm and concern. "No rough stuff," he was saying, his voice like a frightened child's. "Very expensive equipment here. Just taking a few pictures, few little pictures . . ."

"Kenny Dantley, you get the hell out of here! What *right* do you think you've got? What right?"

He looked at her. She was wearing a brilliant red wetsuit, half unzipped. She was partially reclining in the tub of water, and she was struggling to stand up and pull off a pair of absurdly large red flippers at the same time, and she was beginning to weep with frustration.

"Dirty movies," Dantley said. "Great."

"It's not a movie, it's a loop! Idiot!"

"No trouble, fella, okay?" The man was gingerly stepping out of the tub, cradling his camera and watching Kenny warily. "We're all friends here, okay? All consenting adults. Besides, the little lady's being paid real well."

Dantley ignored him, resisting a powerful urge to seize the camera and smash it to pieces on the tiled

153

floor. Instead, he reached down and grasped Vanessa's arm, lifting her—and a great deal of water—out of the tub and onto the bathroom floor. "You're checking out," he said. He marched her back through the bedroom, pausing only long enough to sweep her clothes from the bed and throw them into her white satchel.

All the way down the hall and into the elevator she shouted at him and pounded his arm, yelling that he had no right, crying, struggling to stay on her feet despite the absurd flippers, telling him that she could make money any way she liked, that she could make more money than he could, cursing, leaving froglike watermarks on the hall carpet. Grimly, Dantley dragged her along—into the elevator, across the lobby to the astonishment and amusement of hotel patrons, and out the front door. Only then, when she saw the Corvette, did she fall silent. For a moment she stared at it, mouth open. "You . . ."

"I got it," he said. "We're going back." And he opened the door and pushed her in.

Only when he turned around did he become aware of the huge form of the Indian doorman blocking his path, and then of the chorus of toots and calls from waiting drivers. The Indian did not look at him; he was looking out over Dantley's head, far over the roofs and across the desert to the line of purple hills. "Looks to me," he said, his voice the peculiarly gripping whisper that Dantley remembered from his first night of searching in Las Vegas, "looks to me like you got what you came for."

"Yeah," Dantley said.

"Found what you been lookin' for."

"Yeah."

"These folks here," the Indian said, gesturing toward the impatient cars without actually looking at them, "I guess they're still looking."

Dantley nodded. "Guess so."

"So, how'd you like to go now and let them get on with it?"

"Glad to," Dantley said. "How'd you like to let me past?"

"Sure," the Indian said, and with a movement that was surprisingly agile and graceful, he moved aside.

They left. Vanessa said nothing until they were out of the city and onto the highway. A sign, *Los Angeles 200*, swept by. "I gather," she said, "that you're unemployed."

He nodded.

"You resigned *formally?*"

He grinned. "Let's just say that I gave my notice." He swung the car off the highway and onto the ramp of a gas station. "Look who's here."

Five very low, heavy Chevies were lined up on the right side of the pumps, each one with its body lowered to the asphalt. Dantley pulled up on the left, and the attendant began immediately to fill his tank. "These guys," he said, motioning toward Tico and his friends. "I try to tell them. I say, look, bring two of those things up here on the other side, that way we fill four at once. Think they do that? Nosir!"

"Style," Tico said, grinning and clapping Dantley on the shoulder. "Ya just can't go through life lettin' people rush ya, man. Now, what is this here? Has that big old van we took you home to turned into a *pumpkin?*" The others were walking happily, disdainfully, around the Corvette, peering inside and underneath it. "And what have we here, my friend? A small rubber *doll?*" Tico's grin was enormous.

"Vanessa," Dantley said. "You've met Vanessa."

"But the last time I met Vanessa, she was not wearing her traveling costume."

Vanessa grimaced and stuck out her tongue at him.

"Classy," Tico said. "I have to admit that you show the promise of acquiring some class, Kenneth my boy. Now, if you can only train yourself to drive this gross machine at a reasonable rate of speed so as not to endanger the life and limb of innocent fellow travelers . . ."

A roar interrupted them, the sound of a very powerful car moving at great speed. Over a low hill in front of the station rocketed a low, gleaming, menacing black Trans Am. Wayne. He shot past the filling station and was several hundred yards up the road before he could react to the glimpse he had caught of the Corvette at the pumps. Then there came the awful squealing of brakes being put on hard.

"I think that's enough gas," Dantley said. "Thanks, and keep the change." He got in and slammed the door. "See you," he said to Tico. Thanks for the other night."

"Stay loose."

"Loose," Dantley said, laughing. He started the car. He felt marvelous. He had never felt better, or calmer, or more a part of the machine he was controlling, or more aware of who he was and what he must do. The immediate future lay crystal clear in front of him; and as for the distant future, well, he wasn't worried about that. Life was *now*, now in this instant as the big Trans Am bucked around in its U-turn, tires smoking, coming back for him, and as he waited with all his senses incredibly alert to see exactly which entrance to the filling station Wayne would choose. Life was closing his cool left hand over the shift lever and dropping it into first, and life was the prospect of pushing this machine to the absolute limits of its capability.

He drew his seat belt across and snapped in into its clasp. "You do the same," he said to Vanessa. "And hang on."

Wayne came up the ramp toward them head-on, thinking perhaps to block their escape by skidding the Trans Am sideways at the last moment. But he waited too long; Dantley chose his time well, and when there was still lots of pavement left to swing around the oncoming car he stepped on the accelerator and the Stingray leaped forward. By the time Wayne had skidded the Trans Am through its U-turn and set off in pursuit, the Corvette was a quarter of a mile ahead of him, headed west.

At the gas pumps, the attendant was still holding Dantley's bills. He was gaping. Tico made a face and turned away from the stench of burned rubber. "Gross, gross," he said, smiling. "Those in control of their destinies have no need of haste."

In the Stingray, Dantley had great need of haste, and the car was giving it to him. It had accelerated fast enough to snap both their heads back against the tapering seats, and to make Vanessa suck in her breath. The speedometer needle was rising like the sweep second hand on a watch—past eighty-five, past ninety, effortlessly past ninety-five. Ahead, the road curved, topped a hill, vanished; behind, the back dot which was the Trans Am had just appeared in the rear-view mirrors.

"Small problem," Dantley said.

"What?" Vanessa was gripping her seat, staring straight ahead.

"I've lost the freeway."

"You *what?*"

"Lost it. I came out of that filling station too fast to read the signs. Why didn't *you* read the signs? Aren't you navigating?"

"Nav . . ."

"Never mind. Anyway, we took a wrong turn. Should have gone farther on the cloverleaf or something. The freeway's over there to the left somewhere. Keep a sharp lookout for signs; there's gotta be a road leading down to it *somewhere* along here!" He slowed a little, looking, and the next time he glanced in the mirror the Trans Am was closer.

"I'm gonna take a chance on the next left," he said. "Hang on!"

The intersection came up fast. Dantley braked, fishtailed, accelerated. There was a sickening instant when the rear end skidded on fresh oil toward the ditch while the wheels spun, but then they caught in dry

157

gravel and the car leaped forward. Wayne was more fortunate; the Trans Am took the corner smoothly, somehow avoiding the fresh oil, so that he gained two or three seconds on Dantley and the gap between them narrowed. By the time they roared past a startled survey crew half a mile down the road, the Corvette was in the lead by only three or four hundred yards. In the Trans Am, Wayne was smiling; he knew even before they passed the sign that said *Quarry. Dead End* that he had Dantley trapped. Already he had pulled a nasty little Walther pistol from the glove compartment and, using his knee and elbow to steer, fitted a clip of bullets into the handle.

Concentrating on the road with its slick patches of oil where fresh repairs had been made, Dantley missed the sign, and he was startled by Vanessa pounding his shoulder. "Dead end!" she was shouting, "Dead end!"

Sure enough, the gates of the quarry loomed up around the next bend, rusted and sagging open in an ominous welcome. They shot through, kicking up a huge cloud of dust behind. *Please*, Dantley was thinking, praying almost, although we had not done that since the wife of a social worker took him to church When he was five years old, *please, let him not block that exit!*

He braked, searching wildly for some shelter. Stones ricocheted off the Corvette's undercarriage, and Dantley knew from the sounds they made exactly which part they were hitting. He cursed—not the car for being too low—but the stones for being too high.

"Put it into four-wheel drive," Vanessa suggested, smiling bleakly.

"Very funny." He took a sharp right turn and came to a lurching stop behind a huge boulder. They waited. Dust swirled and settled everywhere.

Wayne came through the gate so fast that the stones rattled, banged and pounded on the undercarriage of the Trans Am. He was halfway to the boulder where the Corvette lurked even before he slowed, and when

158

he caught sight of the familiar red tail he had to brake hard. The nose of the Trans Am went down, plucking at ridges and hillocks of stone, and the car swerved sideways. Even before it had come to a complete stop, Wayne was climbing out of it bringing up the pistol in both hands. The first shot nipped out a corner of the Corvette's left taillight, and would have pierced the car from one end to the other had it not already been moving. The next shot missed altogether, picking out a thumbnail piece of the boulder just above where the red hood was reappearing on the right side, but the next shot knocked off a rear-view mirror. Sun flashed off the windshield into Wayne's eyes then, and in a moment of fright when he could not see and thought that the Stingray was almost upon him, he squeezed off three more shots in quick succession, the Walther kicking in his hands like a small animal straining for release, and all three shots went wild. Then the dazzling light glanced away, and there was only the brilliant red shape of the Stingray itself stretching for the opened gate and freedom. Wayne swung, fired, saw a hole appear in the side rear window, fired again, missed, cursed, fired again, aiming carefully right at the back of Dantley's head, missed again and saw the bullet pick out a groove in the molding around the rear window. By this time the Corvette was through the gate and moving directly away from him, and Dantley was furiously spinning its wheels to raise as much dust as possible. The cloud obscured Wayne's view. Cursing, he jumped back into the Trans Am and took off in pursuit. He was shaking with rage and, though he did not admit it to himself, a little fear. There was the chance, after all, that this kid might just make it. He dropped the almost-spent clip out of the Walther, found another, and fitted it in.

In the Stingray, Vanessa was also shaking. "They were real bullets!" she was saying. "Holy shit! He's trying to *kill* us!"

"Yeah," Dantley said. Ahead of him the survey crew

159

scampered for the protection of the ditches, and he swept past, fishtailing at seventy-five. He was very calm. He knew that in a straight run, on the freeway, he could easily outdistance the Trans Am; *but where was the freeway?*

At the next interesection he turned left, fishtailed down a half-mile of narrow asphalt, ignored the STOP sign, and crashed through the flimsy, weatherbeaten barrier at the end. There it was: the freeway, arrow-straight as far as he could see, and as smooth as the top of a tycoon's desk. Laughing, he accelerated, and the car responded with a high-pitched whine of delight, providing the power he asked for—all the power he would need to outrun the Trans Am, and more.

And yet, something was wrong. No sooner had he glanced into the rear-view mirror and seen the snout of the Trans Am lurch through the shattered barrier a hundred yards behind than he realized they were alone. They were utterly alone. There was no traffic in either direction. And then he understood what he had found—not the main freeway but an unfinished artery leading into the mountains. And he could not crash through, because on the far side there would be tons of rubble and construction machinery. He was on a road to nowhere, and there was no way back.

Suddenly he had a vivid sense of *déjà vu*. He knew that, in the same dreamlike slow motion, he had driven this eerie road before, in the same car, beside the same woman. He had looked out on the same desolate landscape through air so clear and under a sun so bright that everything was bleached, parched, blank as the pages in a child's new coloring book. And although he could clearly see his speedometer registering over one hundred miles an hour, it seemed that he and his pursuer were caught in slow-motion and condemned to play this scene forever.

Then reality returned. It took the form of the black snout of the Trans Am probing up very close, until it almost filled his rear-view mirror. For an instant he regarded it dispassionately, critically. "Ugly," he muttered. "Very ugly."

"I'll say," Vanessa replied. Her voice was a little girl's. She had passed beyond fear. She sat staring straight ahead, shivering a little in her wet rubber suit, hugging her knees in a tight fetal position.

Dantley pushed the accelerator down, down, and the big car surged forward. The Trans Am diminished to a more agreeable size in the mirror, and then it diminished again, until it was only barely recognizable as a car.

Dantley had begun to laugh quietly to himself. He knew now what he would do, and he had actually begun to look forward to the end of the road; that, finally, was the place where he would stop running.

It came two miles farther on, a heavy chain-link fence, securely locked and barred. Dantley reacted fast. There was a small driveway beside the barrier. He swung into this, reversed, and headed back, accelerating, the way he had come. The Trans Am was a quarter of a mile away and coming at at least ninety-five. In no time the Corvette had reached the same speed, and the two cars hurtled toward each other.

"Chicken?" Vanessa screamed, her eyes wide. "You're playing *chicken?*"

"I'm not playing anything," Dantley said. "I'm just going to Los Angeles." The Corvette roared up the center of the road like a big red lion, its great tires gripping firmly.

And now it was Kenny Dantley who was the hunter, because the Corvette was moving on the Trans Am's half of the road, and its pointed snout was aimed dead at the license plate of the other car. Wayne held his position for a few seconds, then wavered, pulling over onto the left side, only to find that the Corvette also pulled over relentlessly. Gasping, Wayne swung back; the Corvette also swung back, absolutely steady, close enough for Wayne to see Dantley's hands on the wheel in the racing driver's traditional grip, and to see Dantley's eyes above the wheel, unwavering.

Wayne panicked. Covering his face, at the last possible instant he pulled his wheel hard to the right, feeling the bumping, jolting, tearing of rocks at the underside of his car, and hearing the awful sound of ripping metal in the seconds before the right wheels hit the soft, deep sand of the ditch and the car was pulled down, and over, and began to turn end over end.

He must have been stunned for only a few seconds, because when he came to, when he had freed his broken leg and dragged himself out of the wreck, he could still hear the triumphant rumble of the Corvette's exhausts receding around the bend in the road. Snarling, discovering the Walther still clutched in his left hand, he fired three futile shots after that sound before swinging the gun on the overturned Trans Am and firing methodically until he hit the gas tank and the machine burst into a belching, searing pyre.

They heard the explosion in the Stingray, and they saw the smoky bloom that rose over the hill behind. Vanessa said, "Aren't you going back?"

Dantley shook his head. "Either he's out or he's not. If he's not, it won't make any difference now."

Later, when they had found the freeway, when the car was purring comfortably, effortlessly at seventy miles an hour, she asked, "Why are you laughing?"

He shrugged. "Lots of things. I just realized that today is the first day of school. We oughtta be going back, right?"

"Wrong," she said. "Never again."

"Just once. What time is it?"

"Seven-thirty."

"We should time it just about right," he said.

Chapter Seventeen

They were a little late. By the time they arrived at MacArthur High classes had already begun. Slowly, carefully, Dantley drove the car over the curb and across the lawn until its nose was almost touching the base of the flagpole. Then he switched off the engine. The only sounds in the silence that followed were the fluttering of the flag, the *pinging* of the metal fastening against the pole, and the voices inside the school, raised in the national anthem.

Vanessa was staring straight ahead, unsmiling. "You're gonna do it, aren't you. You're *really* gonna do it."

"Looks like it."

"You nearly get us both killed so you can *give* the car to the school?"

"It's theirs. I'm just bringing it back."

"It's not theirs. They gave up, remember? It's yours. You designed it, you built it, you found it, you got it away from that bunch of hoods. It's yours. Take it."

"I told you." Dantley spoke very slowly, very deliberately, frowning slightly. "Thing is, if I take it, I won't be any different from them, will I? I'll be a thief. Well, I spent a couple of days being the same as them and I didn't like it. Neither did you."

"It's different."

"It's not different."

"Well *look* at you. You're a mess! Dirty shirt, ripped jeans, grungy sneakers . . . Damn it, Kenny, the car is all you've *got*, and you're going to give it away."

163

He shrugged, grinning. "Thing is, I'm not so sure it's all I've got anymore."

"Well, don't be too sure about me, if that's what you mean. If you give this car away you're a *loser*, and I . . ."

He turned to face her. "Do you really think that?" And when, after a moment, she shook her head, he climbed out of the car and went through the front door of the school. A moment later the fire alarm went off, and he strolled back out. Following him came lines of students, well drilled in fire procedures from the previous year.

Kuchinsky, who had grown even plumper over the summer, was among the first out. When she saw the Stingray and Kenny, she stopped dead in her tracks, hands to her face, indifferent to the others who bumped and pushed her from behind. "You *did* it," she shouted. "You found it!" She flung her arms around his neck and kissed him.

Kootz was close behind her. "Jeez," he said, awestruck. "Holy Jeez."

"Hey, Kootz."

"Hey, Kenny. Hey, my quarter. Didja spend it on the slots like I told you?"

"Yeah."

"Win?"

"Won."

Laughing, they slapped each other's hands.

"Wait'll Ricci hears about this," Kootz shouted. "Hey, listen, Ricci's got a *job*."

"Great," Dantley said, but his mind was not on Ricci. He was watching McGrath and Redman, who had come through the front doorway together, and who had seen the car and him at the same time. He was too far away to hear what Redman was saying to McGrath, but he could guess: "I thought you *fixed* it!" And he could imagine also McGrath's response: "Yeah, Forrie, I thought I did too!"

The car was surrounded by students touching it,

gaping at the bullet holes, and peering inside at Vanessa, who was methodically gathering her things into her handbag. To reach Dantley and the car, Mr. Bacon had to push his way through an assembly of teachers and students ten or twelve deep.

"Hi," Dantley said. "Just thought I'd drop this back to you."

"Kenny! For heavens sake! But you should have *told* us that you found the car. You know, there are proper procedures for this sort of thing."

"No, I didn't know, Mr. Bacon, but here it is anyway, okay?"

"Yes. Of course. Where . . ."

"Vegas."

"But how did you . . ."

Dantley was staring straight at McGrath and Redman, who had drawn closer to listen. "Let's just say I found it," he said.

"Have you told the police?"

"Nope. They don't know a thing about it. They gave up, remember?"

Mr. Bacon looked at him for a long moment, frowning. "Well," he said finally, "I guess I can look after all of that." He turned and began to herd the crowd back inside. "All right. Fire drill's over."

"Mr. Bacon?"

"Yes, Kenny."

"One thing: I'd like my diploma now."

The principal nodded. "I'll send someone to get it."

When the crowd had thinned, Vanessa got out, pulled her handbag after her, and with as much dignity as she could muster in the red wetsuit, went into the school to change. And a few minutes later, only McGrath and Dantley were left beside the Stingray.

"Why?" McGrath asked. "I thought it was all set. All fixed?"

Dantley said nothing.

"You didn't like the money? You didn't get along with Wayne? Why didn't you *call* me instead of . . ."

165

He gestured at the car and the front lawn. He was unable to return Dantley's gaze. "What do you *want*, Kenny? More money? Another car? A new job? I can get you . . ."

Dantley spoke then for the first time. "I don't want anything like that," he said.

Kootz emerged from the school bearing Dantley's diploma, which he presented with a bow and a flourish. It was a tight little roll, secured with ribbon. "You could buy it, you know. It's practically your car. You built it."

"Nahh."

"Why not—it's a terrific street machine! Candy-apple metal flake! Bowtie taillight! Right-hand drive!"

"You buy it, Kootz." Dantley brushed his hand over the top of Kootz's head and down his face. Then he reached inside the Corvette and withdrew a brown envelope—which McGrath recognized immediately—from behind the driver's seat. Vanessa strolled out of the school and joined him. The wetsuit had disappeared: she was wearing a plain top plain jeans. Dantley tapped the roof of the car once with the rolled diploma, and they walked away together without looking back, across the lawn, across the sidewalk. On the boulevard they had to wait for a truck to pass, a huge purple-black Kenworth cabover. Dantley waved to the gnomelike figure behind the wheel, and got a prolonged blast of the air horn in reply. Then he and Vanessa crossed the street.

When McGrath saw them last they were side by side, laughing. He shook his head bitterly. "Dumb kid," he said, turning back into the school. "Hasn't got a thing in the world. Threw it all away."

SIGNET Bestsellers You'll Want to Read

☐ **TWINS by Bari Wood and Jack Geasland.**
(#E8015—$2.50)

☐ **THE KILLING GIFT by Bari Wood.** (#J7350—$1.95)

☐ **KID ANDREW CODY AND JULIE SPARROW by Tony Curtis.** (#E8010—$2.25)*

☐ **OPERATION URANIUM SHIP by Dennis Eisenberg, Eli Landau, and Menahem Portugali.** (#E8001—$1.75)

☐ **'SALEM'S LOT by Stephen King.** (#E8000—$2.25)

☐ **THE SHINING by Stephen King.** (#E7872—$2.50)

☐ **THE MESSENGER by Mona Williams.** (#J8012—$1.95)

☐ **THE FOG by James Herbert.** (#E8174—$1.75)

☐ **THE SURVIVOR by James Herbert.** (#J8369—$1.95)

☐ **CEREMONY by Leslie Marmon Silko.** (#J8017—$1.95)

☐ **EARTHSOUND by Arthur Herzog.** (#E7255—$1.75)

☐ **AZOR! by Jim Henaghan.** (#E7967—$1.75)

☐ **THE FOURTH MAN by Lou Smith.** (#E7880—$1.75)

☐ **THE BLOOD OF OCTOBER by David Lippincott.**
(#J7785—$1.95)

☐ **TREMOR VIOLET by David Lippincott.** (#E6947—$1.75)

☐ **THE VOICE OF ARMAGEDDON by David Lippincott.**
(#E6949—$1.75)

☐ **LAUNCH! by Edward Stewart.** (#J7743—$1.95)

☐ **"THEY'VE SHOT THE PRESIDENT'S DAUGHTER!" by Edward Stewart.** (#E5928—$1.75)

☐ **BAD MOON RISING by Jonathan Kirsch.**
(#E7877—$1.75)

☐ **THE DESPERATE HOURS by Joseph Hayes.**
(#J7689—$1.95)

*Price slightly higher in Canada